Richard Garnett

**Life of Thomas Carlyle by Richard Garnett**

Richard Garnett

**Life of Thomas Carlyle by Richard Garnett**

ISBN/EAN: 9783743306240

Manufactured in Europe, USA, Canada, Australia, Japa

Cover: Foto ©Raphael Reischuk / pixelio.de

Manufactured and distributed by brebook publishing software
(www.brebook.com)

Richard Garnett

**Life of Thomas Carlyle by Richard Garnett**

# LIFE

OF

# THOMAS CARLYLE

BY

RICHARD GARNETT, LL.D.

---

LONDON

## WALTER SCOTT

24 WARWICK LANE, PATERNOSTER ROW

1887

# CONTENTS.

## CHAPTER I.

## CHAPTER II.

## CHAPTER III.

### CHAPTER IV.

### CHAPTER V.

## CHAPTER VI.

## CHAPTER VII.

## CHAPTER VIII.

## CHAPTER IX.

# NOTE.

————

THE duty of acknowledging assistance derived from literary sources is very generally spared to the authors of this series by the copious bibliographies which constitute one of its distinctive features. By these the courteous reader may conjecture what the writer must have read, and the critical reader may discover what he has omitted to read. Some special services, nevertheless, claim special expressions of gratitude. While in no respect responsible for any of the author's statements or opinions not directly quoted from himself, Professor Masson has laid him under the deepest obligation for help and counsel. To Mr. Alexander Ireland, another old and faithful friend of Carlyle's, the writer is indebted for his perusal of the proof-sheets, and for the loan of a copy of the "Reminiscences," in which the innumerable errors of the first edition, only within these last few days superseded by Professor Norton's, were carefully corrected by Mr. Ireland's own hand. Mr. Leslie Stephen's article in the "Dictionary of National Biography" has proved most serviceable as a luminous digest of the subject. Lastly, the author's thanks are due to the kind friend who has relieved the biographer of a Prophet of the secular and sublunary task of compiling an index.

# LIFE OF CARLYLE.

## CHAPTER I.

THOMAS CARLYLE was born at Ecclefechan, in the district of Annandale and county of Dumfries, "in a room inconceivably small," Dec. 4, 1795; four months before Napoleon Bonaparte went forth to conquer, and seven months before Robert Burns ceased to breathe. The hamlet, depicted as "Entepfuhl" in "Sartor Resartus," is not ranked among the beauties of Scotland; he was to inhabit both cities and wildernesses more in harmony with the rugged grandeur of his genius. But he was within hearing of the two mighty voices of Nature, for the Solway Frith ebbs and flows within six miles, and a short walk brings the Cumberland mountains within sight. A few miles further south would have made him an Englishman. This neighbourhood may not have been without influence on his character, since the turbulent times of border raiding are affirmed to have impressed a peculiar wildness of disposition on the folk from whom he sprung. One of his own ancestors was reported to have been unjustly (perhaps justly) hanged for cattle-stealing. These progenitors derived their name, possibly their blood, from a noble but decayed family, originally

English, but domiciled in Scotland since the days of David the Second. The old stock had disappeared, and it was uncertain whether the straggling remnants of the name were offshoots or merely parasites.

Carlyle was the eldest of nine children. His father, James Carlyle, was a mason, who with his own hands had built the house in which his son was born. The fact stamps the man, sturdy, self-reliant, "wholly a man of action, with speech subservient thereto." Stern and rugged, not stolid or sordid. On the contrary, though grimly taciturn, "his heart as if walled in," he seems to have had an instinct of a sphere of light and truth to which he felt forbidden even to aspire. Dissatisfied with the standards of the people around him, he joined himself to a small dissentient sect. With better education he would probably himself have been a minister; as it was, he kept his minister in awe. " Pay the hireling his wages, and let him go!" His vividness of speech, "full of metaphor, though he knew not what metaphor was," warrants the conclusion that his son's genius sprang rather from the father's than the mother's side of the house. Margaret Aitken, the mother, pious, fond, and anxious, "with whom alone my heart played freely," is ever seen throbbing with tender agitation over her son's interests temporal and eternal. She has absolute faith in his ability, yet wonders why he is so slow turning it to account; as a Calvinist she is certain that Tom's fate has been fixed from eternity, and as a mother is equally sure that he may go to heaven if he will. Nothing is more touching than the father's picture of the good woman, "so slow a writer" that she cannot compass a letter to her son during the two days that the carrier stays in the village. She afterwards learned writing on purpose to write to him. It will be readily believed that the family correspondence exhibits the little clan on its most favourable side, and that its lantern of love did not invariably shine before men. Late gleaners of village gossip would persuade us that it had in some respects but an evil report, which probably means no more than was meant by Carlyle when he said, "A kindred warmly liked by those near it, by those at a distance viewed as something dangerous to meddle with." More, indeed, of the old lawless element survived in some of them than in his God-fearing parents. The grandfather had been wild and careless of his family. In his old age he came to live under his son's roof, and one of Carlyle's earliest recollections was of a visit paid to the old man on his death-bed by a long-estranged but now reconciled brother, the retired commander of a revenue cutter; "a grim, broad, to me almost terrible man, so unwieldy that he could not walk. He went away with few words, but with a face that still dimly haunts me, and I never saw him more."

Few anecdotes are recorded of Carlyle's infancy. He had not said a word until, at the age of eleven months, hearing a child cry, he amazed the household by asking, "What ails wee Jock?" He was himself almost always crying, as he informed Professor Masson. Another peculiarity was his constant preference for the company of grown-up people. His first recollection was his mother's intense grief for the death of his infant sister. The indivisible short-clothes suit of yellow serge, immortalized in " Sartor Resartus," was historical; historical too, no doubt, was Teufelsdröckh's reminiscence, how "Many a sunset have I, looking at the distant western mountains, consumed, not without relish, my evening meal. Those hues of gold and azure, that hush of World's expectation as Day died, were still a Hebrew Speech for me ; nevertheless, I was looking at the fair illuminated Letters, and had an eye for their gilding." The influences of Nature thus played their part in shaping his character : the sum of his moral training is stated by himself " We were all particularly taught that work (temporal or spiritual) was the only thing we had to do, and incited always by precept and example to do it well." He is unfortunately obliged to add : " An inflexible element of authority surrounded us all." It was not a joyous life. With many it would not have been what Carlyle declares it was to him, a wholesome one. But filial reverence was ingrained in his nature, and he seems never to have felt the least temptation to disobedience, much less revolt. His obligations to his parents were indeed not ordinary. His mother taught him to read; his father imparted all the arithmetic he knew himself. At five he went to the village school, and at seven was reported "complete in English. I must go to Latin or waste my time." But the schoolmaster himself had never "been to Latin." "Pulled afloat" by the pastor and his son, Carlyle was sent at nine to Annan Grammar School, against the advice of a neighbour in whom the elder Carlyle had much confidence, who said, "Educate a boy, and he grows up to despise his ignorant parents." His father told him this long afterwards,

adding, "Thou hast not done so, God be thanked for it."
"With a noble faith," says Carlyle, "he launched me
forth into a world which he himself had never been
permitted to visit:" thereby, little as he knew it, influ-
encing the world more powerfully than men of five
hundred times his attainments have been able to do.
The beginnings were hard. It was quickly discovered
that the new scholar was shy and sensitive. "The coarse
unguided tyrannous cubs" fell upon him as the young
patricians of Eton fell upon Shelley, and with the more
zest as his hands were tied by a pledge against fighting
given to his mother. When at last the pledge was forgotten under the pressure of intolerable suffering, one
encounter "lifted him from the tribe of Issachar."
But he quitted Annan school with no regret, though with
some obligation for the knowledge he had acquired—
"Latin and French read with fluency, some geometry,
algebra, arithmetic thoroughly well, vague outlines of geo-
graphy. All the books I could get were also devoured."
Among them he afterwards particularly recollected
"Roderick Random," could remember the day and hour
when he read it, the mossy bank on which he sat, the
golden rays of the setting sun. A year afterwards Robertson's preliminary dissertation to his Charles V. delighted
and amazed him, opening "new worlds of knowledge,
vistas in all directions."

It was on November 9, 1809, that Carlyle, wanting
one month of fourteen, finished his eighty miles' walk
from Ecclefechan to Edinburgh, performed to the accompaniment of the perpetual whistling of Tom Smail, an
older but not a wiser lad. Of the impressions which

Edinburgh made upon him, he only distinctly records
that of the law courts, thronged with a buzzing crowd,
which the inexperienced rustic reckoned by the thousand.
But he must have been deeply impressed by the picturesqueness of the most romantic of cities, the old castle
and palace, and the winding ways between them, the
many-storied houses, packed with human beings, the
massive magnificence of the New Town, above all, the
surprised ecstatic feeling, not to be blunted by repetition,
of him who ascends the Castle or the Calton Hill,
to find the unexpected sea at his feet.   Nor have we
any such glowing sketch of his university life as he must
have left if he had been domiciled in an Oxford or
Cambridge college, and had identified his own existence
with its venerable precincts.   The stones of Edinburgh
University have no power to awake romantic sympathy;
her spell consists, or may consist, in a yet nobler instrument, the living voice.   Carlyle might have found himself
sooner, if he had there found a Fichte.   His conception
of a University was august.   "It was for religion," said
he, afterwards, "that universities were first instituted;
practically for that, under all changes of dialect, they
continue; pious awe of the Great Unknown makes a
sacred canopy, under which all has to grow.   All is lost
and futile in universities if that fail."   The young trans-
cendentalist could find nothing congenial in the lectures
of the professor of philosophy, Thomas Brown, though
Brown, an acute metaphysician, was a man of decided
merit in his own way.   Christison, the Latin professor,
never could distinguish the dark slim youth from a
namesake, "with red hair, wild buck teeth, a scorched

complexion, and the worst Latinist in the class." This
was too bad, for Carlyle's progress in Latin was considerable, though his was not the mind to appreciate Horace
and Cicero. Greek, to his life-long prejudice, never became familiar to him. The only professor "who had
some genius in his business," *i.e.*, who saw anything in
Carlyle, was Leslie, the mathematician, who naturally
thought the best he could do for his pupil was to
make him a mathematician also. "He awoke," says
Carlyle, "a certain enthusiasm in me;" the ardent seeker
for truth, moreover, could not but be attracted by the
one science that could claim to be infallible. Useful,
however, as mathematical study doubtless proved as a
discipline, it could not be the task of his life. Carlyle's
human sympathies and interest in the deeper speculative
problems led him to the regions where things must be
seen, not proved; and his love for mathematics gradually
waned, while he preserved so much veneration for mathematical truth as to always pride himself upon the essay
on "Proportion," contributed some years later to his
translation of Legendre. "As good a substitute for the
fifth book of Euclid," says De Morgan, "as could be
given in speech, and quite enough to show that he
would have been a distinguished teacher and thinker in
first principles."

The object of Carlyle's matriculation at Edinburgh—
very definite in his father's mind, considerably less definite
in his own—had been to qualify himself for the ministry
of the Kirk. By the time of his departure in 1814, this
purpose was half abandoned. "My sentiments on the
clerical profession," he writes to his friend Mitchell, on

October 18, 1814, "are, like yours, mostly of the un-
favourable kind. Where would be the harm should we
both stop?" On December 11, 1815, he says: "I have
almost come to a determination about my fitness for the
study of Divinity." The final decision was made in
March, 1817, when Carlyle, calling in Edinburgh to pay
the annual fee for enrolment in the Divinity Hall, and
finding the official absent, "allowed the last feeble tatter
of connection with clerical outlooks to fall definitely to
the ground." His determination was the only sorrow
he ever occasioned his parents, and it was a very severe
one. But they respected his scruples, and abstained
from all endeavours to overcome them.

In the interim Carlyle, like most aspirants to the ministry in Scotland, had been earning his bread as a teacher.
In the summer of 1814, a recommendation from Professor
Leslie had obtained for him, after competition with
another candidate, the post of mathematical teacher in
Annan Academy, at a stipend of £70 a year, "a situation
flatly contradictory to all ideals or wishes of mine." He
nevertheless did the duties manfully, and earned praise as
"a clear and correct expositor." His demeanour to his
pupils is variously reported; *subjectis pepercit ac superbos
debellavit*, most probably. Of his own studies we know
from himself that he would sit up till three in the morning
invincibly tearing his way through Newton's "Principia,"
"without outlook or wish almost, except to master it."
From this time light is cast on his inner life by his
letters to his friend Robert Mitchell, another puzzled
probationer trying to keep out of the Church, in which
aim he likewise succeeded. He died a master of Edin-

burgh Academy in 1836. James Johnstone and Thomas Murray were in due course added to the list of his correspondents. Mitchell was evidently a man of ability. Johnstone, afterwards a schoolmaster, was "not very gifted, but very much attached to me." Murray, by turns clergyman, printer, and newspaper editor, was "a cheery, kindly youth." Carlyle's letters, as Professor Masson remarks, "are wonderful to have been written in the late teens and early twenties of a Scottish student's life." They reveal the innate endowment of original, felicitous metaphor, a sure token of genius, says Aristotle, for it cannot be taught. "In the midst of the kitchen, like a breathing iceberg, stood our guard." Sarcastic pungency was not absent; he thus delivers himself concerning Lord Chesterfield: "His directions concerning washing the face and paring the nails are indeed very praiseworthy." The progress of his mind as exhibited in this correspondence is steady; not slow, but manifesting more bottom than speed; unhasting, unresting. Imaginative literature pleased without enthralling him; his appreciation of Shakespeare is less enthusiastic than it was to become; he is not yet under the spell of a favourite writer, though at this time, as he told Emerson at Craigenputtock, Rousseau's "Confessions" discovered to him that he was not a dunce. Fifteen years afterwards Emerson heard the same acknowledgment from the lips of George Eliot.

An event of great importance to Carlyle occurred in the autumn of 1816, his removal from the academy at Annan to the mastership of a school in Kirkcaldy, a town by the Fife sea-shore. Here, for the first time, he came into intimate contact with a remarkable man, trying to live an intellectual life. Edward Irving, three years and four months older than Carlyle, had been the prize and show pupil of Annan School just before Carlyle entered it—" Trismegistus Irving, a victorious bashaw." He had become master of Kirkcaldy Grammar School, and incurred censure for excessive severity to his pupils: though, even in this age of hero-worship, no one has claimed the honour of having been caned by him. Whatever may have inspired the thought of buying out the old parish dominie and starting an opposition school to Irving's, the project became a fact. The idea of importing Carlyle as the apostle of indulgence confounds our present lights: but the recommendations of Professors Leslie and Christison secured him the post, and he went conquered in advance by the chivalrous generosity of his rival. "You are coming to Kirkcaldy to look about you in a month or two," said Irving when they accidentally met at Annan. "My house and all that I can do for you is yours; two Annandale people must not be strangers in Fife!" "Blessed conquest of a friend in this world!" comments Carlyle. "That was mainly all the wealth I had for five or six years running, and it made my life in Kirkcaldy a happy season in comparison, and a genially useful." Irving proved sagacious, honest-hearted, good-humoured, not without symptoms of a certain "inflation or spiritual bombast," portentous of disaster. His great value to Carlyle was that he consciously, too consciously, stood aloof from and above the things for which Carlyle did not care, and gave the sympathy for want of which many

a pursuer of spiritual things has turned back. " But for
Irving I had never known what the communion of man
with man means." Glorious colloquies they had on the
beach at Kirkcaldy, "a mile of the smoothest sand, with
one long wave coming in gently, steadily, and breaking
in gradual explosion accurately, gradually, into harmless
melodious white, at your hand all the way; the break
of it rushing along like a mane of foam, gradually
sounding and advancing." Next to the stimulus of
Irving's conversation was the access to books which
his friendship opened up to Carlyle. The latter had
meant to immerse himself in mathematics. " I would
study, I thought," he tells Mitchell, "with great vehemence
every night, and the two hours at noon which I have to
dispose of I would devote to the reading of history and
other lighter matters. But alas! two hours I found to be
insufficient—by degrees poor Wallace was encroached
upon, and is now all but finally discarded." Gibbon's
history " was of all the books the most impressive on me
in my then stage of investigation and state of mind.
His winged sarcasms, so quiet and yet so conclusively
transpiercing and killing dead, were often admirable,
potent, and illustrative to me." Gibbon must have done
more for Carlyle than merely unsettle his opinions. Carlyle
must have learned from him how great a thing history is,
and have remarked how much greater Gibbon himself
would have been if his moral enthusiasm had been more
nearly on a par with his industry and his artistic skill. It
was Carlyle's mission to combine all these things; and
the hours when he devoured Gibbon in Irving's study
mark the time when he first consciously turned aside
from abstract science to humanity.

Here, for the first, and with one great exception the
last time, we have a hint of a tender feeling on Carlyle's
part to a woman not of his own kin.  His regard for
Margaret Gordon, the "Blumine" of "Sartor Resartus,"
would, we are assured, have resulted in an engagement
but for the interposition of her friends.  As usual with
Carlyle's admirations, it was called forth by genuine
qualities in its object.  Margaret must have possessed
rare insight to recognize so accurately the gifts and the
genius, the strength and the weakness, of the obscure
young schoolmaster who had not yet written a line.
"Cultivate," she says, in a farewell letter, "the milder
dispositions of the heart.  Subdue the mere extravagant
visions of the brain.  Genius will render you great.
May virtue render you beloved !  Remove the awful
distance between you and ordinary men by kind and
gentle manners.  Deal gently with their inferiority, and
be convinced that they will respect you as much and like
you more.  Why conceal the real goodness that flows in
your heart?"  Miss Gordon was only an occasional visitor
to Kirkcaldy, and Carlyle now lost sight of her.  She
became Lady Bannerman, wife of the Governor of Nova
Scotia.  Carlyle met her once again about 1840, riding
in Hyde Park, "when her eyes (but that was all) said to
me almost touchingly, 'Yes, yes, that is you.'"

"The communion of man with man," as practicable
at Kirkcaldy, came to an end with Irving's departure in
1818, which, added to "some convincing proofs of un-
popularity," made Carlyle exclaim, "I must cease to be
a pedagogue."  His resignation was tendered on
October 23rd, and "a very kind and worthy banker,"

Mr. Swan, having failed in securing his continuance by a subscription, he departed for Edinburgh with very indefinite prospects. He studied the uninviting science of mineralogy, an enterprise soon abandoned, but of infinite importance to him, since for its furtherance he made his first step in German. He earned a pittance by private lessons and translating scientific pamphlets from the French; and his father having now taken a farm at Mainhill, near Ecclefechan, he drew monthly rations of oatmeal and butter from the domestic store. His family wondered and disapproved, but did not remonstrate; he could only comfort them by the assurance that he was "a stubborn dog," and would eventually get Fortune under him. He would not really have been worse off than many another struggling young Scot but for a terrible enemy, which continued to be the scourge of his life. Dyspepsia, probably occasioned by his long fasts and irregular meals, clutched him with a cruelty equal to that which had driven Coleridge and De Quincey to opium. It was as if a rat were always gnawing at the pit of his stomach. Carlyle sought no more perilous anodyne than tobacco, which he was by and bye informed was the occasion of the whole mischief. ("Gave it up, and found I might as well have poured my sorrows into the long hairy ear of the first jackass I came upon as of this select medical man.") He took mercury besides, and castor oil in incredible quantities. Incessant agony aggravated to desperation the wretchedness he was already enduring from "eating of the heart, misgivings as to whether there shall be presently anything else to eat, disappointment of the nearest and dearest as to the hoped-for entrance on the ministry, and steadily-growing disappointment of self—above all, wanderings through mazes of doubt, perpetual questionings unanswered." Thus buffeted between the blue devil and the black, the summer he spent at home was one of the most wretched periods of his life : he could neither read nor think, but ranged the moors in distraction, an object of pity and amazement to his family, who wisely forbore to disquiet him. On his return to Edinburgh he tried law, for the characteristic reason that no mean compliances were requisite for prospering in it : but speedily abandoned it on the equally characteristic ground that it offered no amends for its miseries except its money. A volunteer notice of Pictet's " Theory of Gravitation," for the *Edinburgh Review*, was not even acknowledged : but help came from Brewster, who, although "on most frugal terms," gave him work for the " Edinburgh Encyclopædia." He wrote sixteen articles altogether, beginning with Montesquieu and ending with Pitt. " Not much money in it, but a certain drill, and, still better, a sense of accomplishing something." He read enormously at the Advocates' Library, "an institution pervaded with complete light," as he told the British Museum commissioners thirty years afterwards; he visited Irving at Glasgow, where, observing the enforced idleness and dangerous discontent of the artizans at that gloomy period of our history, he unconsciously laid up thoughts profitable for his future works; and spent much time at Mainhill, outwardly studying, inwardly " living in a continual indefinite pining fear." So passed most of 1820 and the first half of 1821. In June of that year came his deliverance, his "Baphometic fire-baptism." Every reader of "Sartor Resartus" remembers Teufelsdröckh's duel with the Everlasting No; how the Everlasting No said, " 'Behold, thou art fatherless, outcast, and the Universe is mine (the Devil's),' to which my whole Me now made answer: ' *I* am not thine, but Free, and for ever hate thee!' " The incident, Carlyle tells us, is literally true, except that it occurred not in the Rue St. Thomas de l'Enfer, but in Leith Walk, as he was going down to bathe on the sands, after three weeks of total sleeplessness. It may be paralleled from the experiences of St. Paul, Mahomet, Luther, and other members of the spiritual family to which he belonged. Were it possible to analyze a mental process thus seemingly condensed into an instant, it might perhaps in Carlyle's case appear to be, that whereas the Everlasting No had harassed him into deeming that his narrow circumstances and physical suffering were as substantial a reality as the intellectual world in which he truly existed, he was surprised by the sudden perception that the latter was the reality and the former the delusion. Such a leap from the reverse conviction was fit to make a man "strong, of unknown strength, a spirit, almost a god." The prosaic explanation which would connect the state of Carlyle's soul with the state of his stomach is confuted by the absence of any improvement in his health at the time, and of any absolute recovery at any time.

One external circumstance, however, may not have been without its influence. Except for domestic affections, and the flitting figure of "Blumine," woman had as yet counted for nothing in his life. A month before the

discomfiture of the "Everlasting No," in an excursion
into Haddington with Irving, he had met Jane Baillie
Welsh.  Of her anon: meanwhile the correspondence
in which they immediately engaged, though at first confined to the subjects of the young lady's studies, shows
on Carlyle's part a vigour and a vivacious interest which
proclaim the new man.  Irving had been Carlyle's fate
in this matter, and unwittingly helped him on still further
by withdrawing about this time to London, as minister
of the Scotch Church in Hatton Garden.  Carlyle thus
obtained a hold upon the world of London, while a
domain was left vacant for him at home.  Some time
previously the two had taken a memorable walk on
Drumclog Moss, a waste of pared bog, haunted with wild
and gloomy Cameronian memories.  There, as with backs
against a dry wall they gazed into the western radiance,
Irving drew from Carlyle the confession, "that I did not
think as he of the Christian religion, and that it was vain
for me to expect that I ever could or should.  This, if it
was so, he had pre-engaged to take well of me, and
right loyally he did so."  They parted friends, going their
respective ways.  Whose face was set Zionward, time
would show.

## CHAPTER II

A BOUT the time that Carlyle freed himself from the grip of the Everlasting No as related above, he mastered the charm that was to endue him with sword of sharpness, shoes of swiftness, and other equipment befitting a hero. He learned German: partly, as we have seen, for the sake of his studies in mineralogy; partly from the interest aroused in him by Madame de Staël's De l'Allemagne; partly, as he afterwards informed Emerson, by the advice of one who told him that he would find in that language what he wanted. Irving got him a dictionary, a grammar had to be procured from London, his kind Kirkcaldy friend Swan imported books for him from Hamburg, a young man named Jardine taught him in return for lessons in French. " I could tell you much," he says in a letter to Murray, dated Aug. 4, 1820, "about the new heaven and new earth which a slight study of German literature has revealed to me." It is not, indeed, the case that direct translation from the German formed any important part of Carlyle's literary work. The benefit lay in the enlargement of his mental horizon by the discovery of a new world of litera-ture, and the suggestion how the literary forms of his own country, too narrow for his genius, might be rendered pliable by the infusion of this freer spirit. It further provided him with a passport to the publishers. Thomas Carlyle the seer was certain of a cold reception, and Thomas Carlyle the historian was by no means certain of a warm one. But Thomas Carlyle the interpreter of German books and German minds need not despair of a public. "Whittaker," wrote Thirlwall to Hare in 1824, "says German tales are now the rage, and he wishes to take advantage of the mania while it lasts."

Carlyle's enthusiasm for German literature, at first well-nigh all-embracing, gradually resolved itself mainly into enthusiasm for Goethe. Except in the capital points of love of efficiency and hatred of anarchy, two men more superficially dissimilar could not well have been found, and the Scotchman's reverence for the German has excited surprise. His own explanation to Emerson was, "His is the only healthy mind, of any extent, that I have discovered in Europe for long generations." There was something more. He honoured Goethe as a deliverer, as one who had given him what he could not have given himself. He needed an example of repose attained through conflict, and he found it in Goethe. In most English minds there either had been no conflict, or there was no repose. Many passages in Goethe's works seem written for him : there is perhaps hardly an error or an injustice in his subsequent life from which the observance of Goethe's precepts against the merely destructive and negative might not have preserved him. But unquestionably the special value of Goethe to Carlyle at this period of his history was not so much ethical as religious. "It can never be forgotten," he afterwards wrote to Goethe, "that to you I owe the all-precious knowledge and experience that Reverence is still possible: that, instead of conjecturing and denying, I can again believe and know." This, and not admiration for Goethe's genius as a poet or artist, made him tell Sterling, "The sight of such a man was to me a Gospel of Gospels, and did verily, I believe, save me from destruction outward and inward." Of poetry, apart from the teaching it might convey, Carlyle was no infallible judge. His criticisms on Wordsworth, Keats, and Shelley could only be described as idle if they had not been a solid piece of the man himself. The ideas did not commend themselves to him, and the witchery of language and music exerted no fascination. "Poetry," he says, "is no separate faculty, no organ which can be superadded to the rest, or disjoined from them, but rather the result of their general harmony and completion." If so, why was not Carlyle himself a poet? He never understood that there is an essence of poetry quite distinct from moral purpose or the knowledge of life; and that if without these things it is but a soul without a body, they without it are but a body without a soul. When, therefore, he apparently puts Goethe so high above his contemporaries, the injustice is less than it seems. He is not really thinking of him as a poet, but as a moral and intellectual force. "It is admirable in Carlyle," said Goethe himself to Eckermann, "that in his judgments of our German authors he has especially in view the mental and moral core." "That poetry which masters write," says Carlyle, "aims at incorporating the

everlasting reason of man in forms visible to his sense."
This definition would have excluded half of Goethe
himself.   Nor did the other half find in him an easy or
submissive conquest.   He was slow to admire " Faust " :
his cavils at "Wilhelm Meister," even while translating it,
anticipate Jeffrey and De Quincey.   Years afterwards he
admitted that he had been long without understanding
what Goethe meant by *Entsagen*.   But he said at the
same time, "I still find more in Goethe than in any
other."

Next to Goethe's, the chief German influence upon
Carlyle was that of Jean Paul, who helped to elicit his
natural gift of humour, and showed him how to press
erratic fancy into the service of reason and truth.   It was
an invaluable lesson, without which Carlyle's vehement
eloquence would more frequently have become, what it
sometimes does become, a mere monotonous preachment.
Richter's influence, nevertheless, rather affected his
manner than his matter, adding the arabesques of German
luxuriance to the concentrated pith of his native Annandale.

Fichte is another great German writer to whom Carlyle's
obligations are very apparent.   "The guiding principle of
all Carlyle's ethical work," says Fichte's interpreter
Professor Adamson, "is the principle of Fichte's specu-
lation, that the world of experience is but the appearance
or vesture of the divine idea or life ; and that he alone
has true life who is willing to resign his own personality
in the service of humanity, and who strives incessantly
to work out the ideal that gives nobility and grandeur to
human effort."   Professor Adamson instances " Sartor

Resartus " and the " Characteristics " as works especially imbued with Fichte's spirit, and it may be added that the concluding lecture of Fichte's "Characteristics of the Present Age" might pass for Carlyle's own, if it had humour and symbol.

The first hint of Carlyle's having "acquired a weak tincture of German" occurs in February, 1819. We have seen that he had learned to prize German literature by August, 1820. In January, 1821, he tells his brother Alexander that he has sent a specimen of a translation of Schiller's "Thirty Years' War " to Longmans. By April, 1822, he deemed that he had sufficiently digested "Faust" to write an essay upon it in the *New Edinburgh Review*. This crude production should be preserved with pious care as the index to a prodigious mental growth. The ideas which he was trying to grasp were for the moment too great for him. He had begun his studies at what would have been the wrong end for an ordinary man. In the same April Shelley wrote a letter on "Faust," imparting in five lines more insight than could have been obtained from five volumes of lucubrations like Carlyle's. But Shelley had begun with Goethe the poet, and found him an alluring introduction to Goethe the thinker. Carlyle had reversed the process. A wider field for literary enterprise was gained for him by Irving. Sterling, not perhaps without playful exaggeration, told Caroline Fox how Irving, being invited to contribute an article to the *London Magazine,* looked into the said magazine and discovered the expression, "Good God !" An atheist could not have been more scandalized. No, it would be impossible for him to have anything to do with it, but he had a friend who was not so scrupulous. The unscrupulous Carlyle consequently began to publish his "Life of Schiller" in this magazine in 1823, thus letting his light shine along with Lamb and De Quincey. The work, published complete in 1825, is termed by the author himself "an insignificant book." It might not have lived without his name, but has the merit of true artistic proportion, and is a sound piece of work, "containing nothing that I did not reckon true, and wanting nothing which my scanty and forlorn circumstances allowed me to give it." It is a pleasure to hunt in it for streaks of the coming Carlyle. The blank verse of the translated passages betrays his fatal deficiency of ear.

"Schiller," wrote Carlyle, while the work was still in progress, "is not in my right vein, though nearer to it than anything I have yet done. In due time I shall find what I am seeking." He found it in "Wilhelm Meister." His translation marks the dividing line between his intellectual boyhood and his adolescence. Another Jacob, he wrestled with Goethe, and would not let him go till he had won his blessing. In September, 1823, he "loves not" Meister; he is sure it will never sell. "Goethe is the greatest genius that has lived for a century, and the greatest ass that has lived for three." In the following January he reports: "Bushels of dust and straw and feathers, with here and there a diamond of the purest water." But by April he is compelled to testify,— "I have not got as many ideas from any book for six years;" and by the time the preface has to be written, the principal demerit is "the disfigurement of a translation." This preface is Carlyle's first piece of work in which his natural and his acquired manner appear thoroughly blended and welded into one. His version was diversely estimated by the critics. Jeffrey disparaged the book, but commended the translation ; *Blackwood* approved both ; De Quincey neither. "A Cockney animalcule !" growled Carlyle ; and though afterwards on pleasant terms with the Opium Eater, he never quite forgave him. The translation brought him £180, and to his good mother the conviction that "foreign persons have exactly the same feelings as ourselves," and that Tom was somebody at last.

To complete the record of Carlyle's translations from the German, mention may here be made of his "Specimens of German Romance," though they were not published till 1827. "A book," he says, "not of my suggesting or desiring, but of my executing as honest journey-work in default of better." It included selections from Jean Paul, Tieck, Fouqué, and Hoffmann ; also the second part of "Wilhelm Meister," in its original form, this last not very interesting reading with the exception of "The New Melusina," but profoundly influential on his life. Leigh Hunt, reporting his lectures delivered in 1839, has preserved the memorable autobiographic passage in which he recounted to the audience his emancipation from "Wertherism"—how he had found in "Wilhelm Meister" that the letters of several young persons who had written for happiness were tossed aside unanswered, and this had struck him as very strange. At last he began to perceive that happiness was not the right thing to seek. The spiritual perfection of his nature, a mystic and nameless aim, but of which, though no man could explain it, they were the only pitiable who had no glimpse, this was the true object of search, and the proper end and aim of life. No wonder that he rated the second part of "Meister" by another standard than its æsthetic worth.

Before Carlyle had begun the translation of "Wilhelm Meister," his destiny had been influenced by the generous interposition of Irving, whose sky-rocket eloquence, like Teufelsdröckh when he fell in love, "was rising to the highest regions of the Empyrean by a parabolic track, to return thence by a perpendicular one." Among its observers were the Bullers, retired Anglo-Indians intent on the education of three promising sons. They had already thought of the University of Edinburgh for the two eldest, and readily fell in with Irving's suggestion that its teaching should be supplemented by private instruction from Carlyle. Carlyle assented, his remuneration was to be £200 a year. The Bullers arrived in August, 1822, just after the publication of the translation of Legendre. The tutor found himself treated with cordial kindness, even made more of than always suited his recluse humour. Mr. Buller, an earnest, sturdy Benthamite, was not a man after his heart, but was one whom he must needs respect. Mrs. Buller, a beauty and woman of the world, "bright, airy, and ardent," tried him by her volatility and whim. The full strength of her feeling was to be shown in after years, when she died broken-hearted at the loss of her brilliant son, Carlyle's eldest pupil. "A most manageable, intelligent, cheery, and altogether most welcome phenomenon," witnesses his tutor, who had written privately, "My pupils behave

extremely well to me and extremely ill to themselves."
When we hear that Charles Buller's principal fault was
then considered to be indolence, and remember that he
lived to frame in conjunction with Edward Gibbon Wake-
field the Durham Report, the charter of Colonial self-
government, and died President of the Poor Law Board,
with his foot on the threshold of the Cabinet, we may
conclude that Carlyle's influence was precisely what he
required. Great part of 1823 was spent at Kinnaird in
Perthshire, where the Bullers had taken a shooting-box,
and where Carlyle could pace the moors when fretted by
Mrs. Buller's domestic management. His perambulations
were many and long. In the early part of 1824 he was
chiefly at Mainhill, finishing his translation of "Wilhelm
Meister," and was at last a little king over his family,
which he most generously assisted out of his improved
means, supporting his brother John as a medical student
at Edinburgh, and stocking a farm for Alexander. "What
any brethren of our father's house possess," he said, "I
look on as common stock, from which all are entitled to
claim whenever their convenience requires it." In June
he followed the Bullers to London, but their frequent
changes of plan tired him out, and he resigned his
tutorship, to the "sadness and anger" of Charles.

From June, 1824, to March, 1825, Carlyle was mainly
in London, with two episodes of excursions to Paris and
Birmingham. He at first saw much of Irving, but
grieved to find him deteriorating in the unwholesome
atmosphere of popular preachership, "sped," as Pope
Alexander said of Savonarola, "with the wind of the
Florentines." Irving had married meanwhile, but his

wife, though Carlyle seems to have unduly disparaged her, brought him no ballast for the voyage of life. The people about him were moreover of a painfully inferior sort; and he had adopted views on the speedy end of the world which might be meat and drink in a very real sense to an impostor, but could only wreck an earnest man. Carlyle found new friends in Mrs. Buller's sister, Mrs. Strachey, and "the noble lady," Mrs. Basil Montagu, whom he evidently admired at the time, and would have continued to admire if others would have suffered him. Mrs. Strachey he never ceased to honour, and wrote of her years afterwards, "She is the same true woman she ever was, indignant at the oppressing of the poor, at the wrong and falsehood with which the earth is filled; yet rather gently withdrawn from it and hoping in what is beyond it than actively warring with it." In her husband, colleague of James Mill and Peacock at the India House, he found a "genially-abrupt man, a Utilitarian and Democrat by creed; yet above all things he loved Chaucer." More famous folk impressed him less. He cursed Lamb with a curse that has come home to roost. Coleridge, whom Shelley had beheld—

> " Obscure
> In the exceeding lustre and the pure
> Intense irradiation of a mind
> Which, with its own internal lightning blind,
> Flags wearily through darkness and despair."

—the iconoclastic Scot pronounced "A steam-engine of a hundred horses' power, with the boiler burst." "He speaks incessantly, not thinking or remembering but combining all these processes into one." About this very time Henry Nelson Coleridge was amassing golden fragments from his uncle's talk, by dint of patient listening and sifting. But Carlyle was hasty and undevout, and not at all disposed to follow Coleridge through mazes of verbiage, as the little boy in the " Mill on the Floss" followed the peacock, in hopes that he would drop a feather from his tail. The great revelation of London to Carlyle, however, was London itself. " It is like the heart of all the universe, and the flood of human effort rolls out of it and into it with a violence that almost appals one's very sense. ' O that our father saw Holborn in a fog ! with the black vapour brooding. over it, absolutely like fluid ink ; and coaches and wains. and sheep and oxen and wild people rushing on with bellowings and shrieks and thundering din as if the earth in general were gone distracted ! Then there are stately streets and squares, and calm green recesses into which nothing of this abomination is permitted to enter. No wonder Cobbett calls the place a Wen. It is a monstrous Wen !" His visits to Birmingham and Paris also were not unimportant to him. At the former place he studied the artizans of whom he was afterwards to write ; at the latter, which he visited with Strachey and Mrs. Strachey's cousin, Miss Kitty Kirkpatrick, he gained an acquaintance with the topography of the city which stood him in good stead when he wrote of the French Revolution. He introduced himself to Legendre ("a tall, bony, grey old man ") on the strength of his translation ; and might, . but for his reserve, have been introduced to Laplace. His family were astounded at his intrepidity.

All the stoutness of their hearts, wrote Alexander, was required to bear it : and, until news of his safety arrived, "the women, if they attempted to sing or indulge in laughing, were reproached with unbecoming lightness of heart." "Do not," his mother entreated, "let me want food. Your father says I look as if I would eat your letters."

On the same day that his mother's yearning found such pathetic voice (Dec. 18, 1824), Carlyle was announcing to his brother John an authentic recognition of his status as man of letters in the shape of a letter from Goethe, acknowledging the translation of "Wilhelm Meister." It was couched in Goethe's stately style, to be quickened by sympathy when the "Life of Schiller" convinced him that Carlyle was more than a mere translator. His line in life seemed clearly marked out for him, yet he halt recalcitrated. Years afterwards he told Professor Masson that he judged himself at bottom less fit for the literary calling than any other, and wrote to Hutchison Stirling that he deemed it as a mere trade "the frightfullest, fatalest, and too generally despicablest of all now followed under the sun." A mere trade it must be for some time under his present circumstances, and there seemed risk of its proving a sorry one. The right relations between himself and the booksellers appeared to him singularly inverted. "They are," he said, "as the packhorses of literature ; which the author should direct with a halter and a goad, and remunerate with clover and split beans. Woe to him if the process is reversed, and he is tied to their unsightly tail." At another time he said, "They want to invest their money to-night and get it back to-morrow

morning." At last, however, arrangements were made
for the translation of "German Romance," and, declining
a proposal from the Bullers to undertake the education
of their second son, afterwards an honoured judge in
India, Carlyle fell in with the offer of his family to take
for him Hoddam Hill, a farm two miles from Mainhill,
which brother Alexander should manage while he fagged
at his German. There he installed himself in March,
1825, and there lived for a time "a russet-coated idyll."
He wrote ten pages of his translation daily, took long
rides on his Irish horse "Larry," and sent his thoughts
on errands through all time and space. The term idyll
is significant : love was now a chief element of his
existence.

Jane Baillie Welsh, to whom, as already mentioned,
Carlyle had been introduced by Irving in 1821, was the
daughter of John Welsh, a surgeon who had died in
1819 from typhus fever, caught in attending a patient.
He had possessed the manor house of Craigenputtock, in
Dumfries-shire; his widow and daughter lived at Haddington. Jane (born July 14, 1801) was beautiful, witty,
and original. Among her father's ancestors was a
daughter of John Knox; her mother claimed descent
from William Wallace. She had learned Latin and
written much poetry ; one remaining piece, composed
however at a later period, is of high quality. Irving had
been her tutor years before, and she had conceived a
childish passion for him. The intimacy had been interrupted by his removal to Kirkcaldy, but had been resumed
after his resignation of his school. Unfortunately he
came back from Kirkcaldy engaged to Isabella Martin,

daughter of the minister of that place. This had to be
owned when he found himself responding to Miss Welsh's
feelings, and the explanation was precipitated by his
departure for London in 1821. She would apparently
have accepted him if the Martins would have released
him, but they held him to his contract, and her reflections
on the incident, as well as the sentimentality and extravagance of his letters from London, soon convinced her
that she had greatly overrated him. "My standard of men
is immensely improved," she says in September, 1824.
Her mind had vastly expanded, and she had found but
one other that could keep pace with it. The warmth of
Carlyle's first letters to her manifests an intellectual
comradeship on very short acquaintance; a tenderer
feeling is soon unconsciously evinced by his deference,
his patience under criticisms which he would have resented from any one else, and his obvious anxiety for
her good opinion. The tale cannot be completely told,
for Professor Norton, the guardian of her letters and
Carlyle's, has not yet seen it right to publish many, and
has only yielded to urgent necessity in publishing any at
all. A significant bubble, however, occasionally comes
up from the deep. In an early note Miss Welsh speaks
of "importunities" which have to be repressed. On
August 19, 1823, she says, "I owe you much; feelings
and sentiments that ennoble my character, that give
dignity, interest, and enjoyment to my life—in return I
can only love you, and *that* I do from the bottom of my
heart." Carlyle, in return, adjures her to think of him
as one whom it is dangerous and useless to love. More
correspondence follows, with a result thus summed up

by Carlyle: "You love me as a sister, and will not wed; I love you in all possible senses of the word, and will not wed any more than you." Matters could not long remain on this basis. Miss Welsh showed her determination to protect Carlyle from all possible misconstruction by executing a deed, transferring to her mother the whole of the property bequeathed to her by her father. She further indicated the state of her feelings by bequeathing it to Carlyle in the event of her own and her mother's death. In the spring of 1824 she brought herself to the point of promising to become his wife if he could achieve independence. By 1825 this prospect seemed no longer so remote. Carlyle thought he could live at Craigenputtock, and farm the property himself. Miss Welsh was ambitious as well as affectionate, and did not relish this apparent descent from her family's quasi-lairdship. She replied drawing a fine distinction between loving Carlyle and being in love with him, and throwing much cold water on the project, which indeed was not judicious. Carlyle answered in a most eloquent letter, but the facts of the case could not be altered. So things drifted on. The inevitable end was accelerated by an interference on the part of Mrs. Montagu, which for the first time informed Carlyle of Irving's former relations with Miss Welsh, and led her to visit Carlyle's family as his promised bride (September, 1825). She was received with simple courtesy, and always remained on affectionate terms with them. Next year Hoddam Hill was given up on account of disagreements with the landlord. The family took a neighbouring farm called Scotsbrig, and Carlyle and his betrothed, weary of lingering in

general unsettlement, agreed to marry and take a cottage
at 21, Comely Bank, Edinburgh, where Carlyle was to
support himself by literary labour. Their prospects might
have been improved if Mrs. Welsh had lived with them;
but the senior lady disliked Carlyle as a person of
questionable principles; she had also been observed to
be in fifteen tempers in one afternoon. Carlyle's objections may have seemed ungracious, but he certainly judged
wisely. The marriage took place on October 17, 1826.

The full history of Carlyle's wooing cannot yet be fully
written. Whether it ought to be may be cheerfully left to
the decision of Professor Norton, the accomplished and
true-hearted editor of his early correspondence, who has
already done much to put the matter in its true light.
Mr. Froude, "coming to bury Cæsar, not to praise him,"
has involved it in a cloud of misrepresentation prejudicial
to Carlyle and his wife also, which is blown away in
Professor Norton's appendix. The idea that Carlyle
acquired any worldly advantage but the distant reversion
to a small property is absurd upon the face of it. The
notion that Jane Welsh made any real sacrifice by the
acceptance of an uncertain prospect is thus negatived by
Professor Masson: "There was nothing extraordinary whatever in the match between the educated son of a Scottish
peasant and the daughter of a Scottish provincial surgeon.
If Jane Welsh had not married Carlyle, and been pro-
moted by that marriage into a sphere far higher in the
world's affairs than would otherwise have been within her
reach, she would have probably lived and died the
equally drudging wife of some professional Scottish nobody."

Carlyle had now won the woman intellectually most suited to him in all Scotland, and after an ordeal which might be thought to have sufficiently tested the worth and congeniality of both. But there are things that cannot be known beforehand. The marriage was doomed to want the blessing of children, and this meant that much indispensable for its happiness, and which happier circumstances would have called forth, must slumber for ever. Thomas Carlyle had an immense fund of spiritual tenderness, but it was so far passive that it did not go forth freely of itself; it needed to be evoked, and then the fountains streamed. Towards the weak and and helpless it flowed freely, but the strong could only elicit it by themselves displaying the like. Jane Carlyle's tenderness of spirit, as distinguished from her sympathizing helpfulness in actual misfortune, was potential; circumstances might have aroused it, but the circumstances never arrived, and the tenderness never awoke. Hence she and Carlyle were in a sense ill-suited; each could give the other what he or she already had, but neither could give what the other wanted. They were like traders bartering the same thing. If Carlyle was ever sour and surly, he found no soother and no monitor in his wife; nor could he, whose better mind was never appealed to by her, exorcise the ill-nature that defaces her brilliant letters. He had done very much for her before marriage, he seems to have been less influential over her afterwards. She comforted him greatly by her steady faith in his genius, but exerted little influence on its productions, unless by encouragement of the negative and sarcastic elements in his nature. There was still much to admire in their loyal alliance and the steadfast valour of their battle with the world; yet, each being so strong without the other, and the help which they might have mutually given remaining to so great a degree dormant, it may be regretted that it was not bestowed where it would have been expended wholly, and expended to better purpose. When poor Irving, oblivious of his Kirkcaldy vows, sought Miss Welsh's hand, he was perhaps guided by a sound instinct of his real needs. "Had I married Irving," she said afterwards, "the 'tongues' would never have been heard." It would have gone much better with Irving, and perhaps not much worse with Carlyle. But we are falling into the vein of Alphonso of Castile, who ventured to think that if he had been consulted on occasion of the creation of the world, the All-Wise might have derived some not unserviceable hints from him, Alphonso.

# CHAPTER III.

IT would ill become the biographer of Carlyle to arraign the dealings of Providence with his hero, for, by a certain divine irony, the foremost preacher and practiser of self-help was above most men aided by allies who seemed especially raised up to succour him. Irving, who could only mar his own destiny, made Carlyle's by helping him to a wife who helped him to a friend in one more likely to have proved a dangerous enemy. Sceptical, superficial Jeffrey, who had modestly undertaken to crush the "Excursion," and in whose ear "Christabel" rang like nursery jingle, takes a more revolutionary innovator than Wordsworth and a more mystical seer than Coleridge by the hand, and accoutres him in the blue-and-yellow uniform of an Edinburgh Reviewer.

Two of Jeffrey's three motives for this enlistment of a recruit, merely recommended to him by Procter out of regard for Mrs. Carlyle, were much to his honour. He felt chivalrously towards Carlyle's wife, and cheerfully admitted her claim to the good offices of a somewhat problematic kinsman. He discerned true metal in Carlyle himself, and, in the third place, had his own theory about him. "The great source," he told him,

"of your extravagance, and of all that makes your
writings intolerable to many, and ridiculous to not a few,
is not so much any real peculiarity of opinions as an
unlucky ambition to appear more original than you are."
In process of time he was obliged to admit that the
disease lay deeper, and that Carlyle actually did hold it
man's duty "to have a right creed as to his relations
with the universe," instead of taking up with "the first
creed that came to hand." Yet even then charity pre-
vailed, and he assured his successor, Macvey Napier,
that Carlyle's articles might be made tolerable by
"striking out and writing in," and that he really
possessed "the capacity of being an elegant and impressive writer." Ludicrous as such judgments must
appear now, it must be admitted that Carlyle's purple
patches contrasted violently with the general texture of
the *Edinburgh*, even with the no less splendid tissues of
Macaulay. Jeffrey's attitude represented the opinions
of the vast majority of his public, and his tolerance and
encouragement, from the editorial point of view unwise,
were all the more spirited and courageous. *Ogni
picciolo sempre ha gran cuore.*

A helping hand was indeed needful. Carlyle, not
unreasonably sanguine in view of his prospects, had
crippled his own means by undertaking to provide for
his brother John's medical education on the Continent.
But the "pack-horses of literature" had turned restive.
"German Romance" did not sell, being found deficient
in *diablerie*. A projected novel confuted Carlyle's
theories of the omnipotence of the human will by ob-
stinately refusing to be written. A prospectus of a

"Literary Annual Register" elicited no response, and the young couple firmly refused the sixty pounds of which Mrs. Welsh wished to deprive herself for their sakes. The *Edinburgh Review* and the newly-established *Foreign Review* came to the rescue of the poor little household at Comely Bank. Jeffrey was in truth benignant and self-sacrificing. He not only let Carlyle write, but let him write on his own particular aversion, German Literature. Years afterwards he congratulated Macvey Napier on having found a new contributor, who, in spite of knowing German and Scandinavian, retained sense, moderation, and judgment. He can hardly have discovered these qualities in the first essay Carlyle wrote for him, on Richter, in whose person the author adumbrated his own; or in the second, on German Literature, invaluable as a profession of faith and as a picture of Carlyle's mind, every phase of which seems to come successively into view as he takes up writer after writer. During his short residence in Edinburgh, Werner, Goethe's Helena, Goethe in general, Heyne, were treated in rapid succession for the *Edinburgh* or the *Foreign Review*. The essay on Heyne manifests Carlyle's craving for concrete realism in biography ; that on the Helena is remarkable for the excellent rendering of the translated specimens. On these we must not dwell, but the next essay, on Burns (December, 1828), revealed Carlyle in his full power and engaged him in a dispute with his editor. Jeffrey, who had already ascended the tripod to predict "with full and calm assurance" that England would never admire or endure Carlyle's German divinities, now informed him that their example had made him "a little verbose and prone to exaggeration. I have tried to staunch the first, but the latter is in the grain." When Carlyle received his proof, he found that, instead of staunching the blood, Jeffrey had amputated the limb. He refused to submit, and the great editor yielded, protesting that he had only wished to serve Carlyle by keeping his mannerism and affectation out of sight. Carlyle's first letter had been defiant. Jeffrey's generosity conquered him, and the "candour and sweet blood" of his reply were repaid in kind. "I cannot," wrote Jeffrey, "chaffer with such a man, or do anything to vex him : and you shall write mysticism for me if it will not be otherwise, and I will print it too at all hazards with very few and temperate corrections." The essay thus saved as by fire is the very voice of Scotland, expressive of all her passionate love and tragic sorrow for her darling son. It has paragraphs of massy gold, capable of being beaten out into volumes, as indeed they have been. Unlike some of Carlyle's essays, it is by no means open to the charge of mysticism, but is distinguished by the soundest good sense. No reasonable account of Burns, or of any other example of noble genius flawed by moral weakness, could be given on any other principle. Knowing of Carlyle himself what we know now, we can see how nearly the subject touched him, and how he felt himself in many things another Burns.

Before this article had been written the Edinburgh house had been given up, and Carlyle and his wife were settled at the Welshes' manor at Craigenputtock, a

lonely farmhouse isolated among miles of dreary moor-
land, seven hundred feet above the level of the sea. "A
solitude altogether Druidical," Carlyle calls it when
urging De Quincey to let him and his helpmate "hear
the sound of philosophy and literature in these hitherto
quite savage wolds, where, since the creation of the
world, no such music, scarcely even articulate speech,
has been uttered or dreamed of." The farm was to be
worked by Carlyle's brother Alexander. Carlyle had
judged wisely for himself: he could hardly have written
"Sartor Resartus" in Edinburgh. From his wife, one is
inclined to say, the sacrifice should not have been exacted;
she resigned all amusements, consigned herself to almost
total solitude, underwent more domestic drudgery than
heretofore, and was not repaid by any extraordinary en-
hancement of her husband's tenderness. "I fancy," he
says of Dante, thinking of himself, "the rigorous earnest
man, with his keen excitabilities, was not altogether easy
to make happy." His affection was, in truth, much
deeper than hers, but he was absolutely incapable of
following Jeffrey's excellent advice, " to be gay and playful and foolish with her at least as often as you require
her to be wise and heroic with you." "You don't want
to be praised for doing your duty," he once said. "But,"
says Mrs. Carlyle, very naturally and prettily, "I did,
though." "In his early years," says Professor Norton,
who knew him at a mellower time of life, "he had not
fully learned the importance to the sum of happiness in
life of frequent and frank expression, in varied mode, of
the sentiment lying at the heart. But bitter experience
taught him, " Give quickly ! " It should be added

4

that the removal was partly forced upon the Carlyles by
their Edinburgh landlord, and that her daughter's neighbourhood was greatly desired by Mrs. Welsh.  The
principal events of their Edinburgh residence had been
the receipt of cordial letters and graceful presents from
Goethe ("the very arrangement and packing of which
we found to be poetic and a study"); more intimate
acquaintance with De Quincey, whom Mrs. Carlyle
nursed in an illness; and unsuccessful endeavours,
backed by Jeffrey, blocked by Brougham, to obtain
for Carlyle a professorship at University College; as
also to pour his new wine into the venerable bottle of
the University of St. Andrews.  He seems to have hoped
to gain a post at the latter seat of learning by means of,
or in spite of, testimonials from the Pantheist Goethe and
the enthusiast Irving.  During his years of struggle it
was a weakness of his to be always wanting something
inappropriate or impossible.  He had himself written—
" A prophet and teacher has no right to expect great
kindness from his age, he is rather bound to do it great
kindness."

The year 1829, uneventful as regarded external incidents, was important for Carlyle's literary history.  Jeffrey,
retiring from the editorship of the *Edinburgh Review*
was succeeded by Macvey Napier, who took Carlyle over
with the other properties, and found him proper for the
shelf.  That Jeffrey actually thought of Carlyle as his
successor is affirmed on the testimony of unpublished
letters, but staggers belief.  The Review was a great
party organ.  Was Carlyle to concert political campaigns
with Brougham and Lord John Russell?  If Jeffrey

devised such destinies for his protégé, the project was
never breathed to those who alone could have made it
a fact. He had just discouraged Carlyle's proposal to
write on Voltaire. On the other hand—as a malefactor
is indulged with a breakfast before he is hanged—
Carlyle was allowed his full fling in "Signs of the
Times" (October, 1829). Here for the first time we
have Carlyle championing spiritual Dynamics against
Mechanics, and denouncing the superstitious belief of
the age in phrases, formulas, outward institutions cor-
responding to no inward conviction, and other contri-
vances for dispensing with the wisdom which is from
above. Carlyle had long been "delivered from this
outwardness," as Caroline Fox says in her pretty Quaker
way. His article brought him epistles and manifestos from
the Saint Simonians, who deemed him the man for them
The essay on Voltaire (*Foreign Review*, April, 1829) is
one of the most remarkable instances of his justice
and penetration. Spiritual power could not present itself
in a form less attractive to him that that of the arch-
scoffer; but there it was, and Carlyle recognized it in the
spirit in which he afterwards wrote to Sterling : " Fear no
*seeing* man. Know that *he* is in heaven, whoever else be
not; that the arch-enemy is the arch-stupid. I call this
my fortieth church article, which absorbs into it and
covers up in silence all the other thirty-nine." Written
in such a spirit, the essay in a measure supersedes all
others on Voltaire. The outward circumstances of his
life and his personal relations to others may still be
profitably investigated; Voltaire the writer may still
repay minute criticism; but Voltaire the man can hardly

be better known. Novalis, apparently a more congenial subject for Carlyle, produced a less satisfactory essay (July, 1829)—valuable, however, as proving what an element of solidity was combined with Carlyle's mysticism. As an oracle Novalis was too enigmatic for him, as a poet too ethereal, as a personality too little known. The biographical details which have since given substance to the portrait were not then accessible. "German Playwrights," written a little earlier, overflows with jocularity, at the expense not merely of such wights as Klingemann, the tragic property-man, and Clotho-Lachesis-Atropos Müllner, but also of Grillparzer, a more considerable dramatist than Carlyle would allow, and whose moral nature rather wanted breadth than toughness.[1]

Carlyle's connection with the *Edinburgh* was not entirely broken off, though he was only to contribute three more articles. Nothing having come of a proposed essay on fashionable novels, he returned to the *Foreign Review*, and enlisted among the recruits of .*Fraser's Magazine*, contributing to the very first number (Feb. 1830). How this came about is not stated, probably through Irving, of whose congregation the publisher

[1] Grillparzer, in whom Carlyle discovered "an amiable tenderness of natural disposition," was accused in his own country of undue self-assertion, and retorted in an epigram which may be thus rendered :

> " Thou thyself art a luminous proof
>      That thy precept is solid and sage :
>    Had'st thou not been a lamb in thy youth,
>       Thou had'st ne'er been a sheep in thine age."

of the Magazine was a member. He began with a translation of Richter's review of Madame de Stael's Germany,
interesting for its resemblance to his own style. Other
minor contributions followed, including Carlyle's solitary prose fiction, "Cruthers and Johnson," written in
1822 or 1823, and in which it is difficult to discover a
trace of his characteristic manner. Another essay on
Richter appeared in the *Foreign Review;* in general,
however, 1830 was an unproductive year, Carlyle's main
energies having been expended in a history of German
Literature, with which no "packhorse of literature"
would burden himself. It ultimately appeared in the
shape of separate articles in the *Foreign* and *Westminster
Reviews.* Carlyle's connection with *Fraser* proved a
signal piece of good fortune. The light monthly encouraged him in audacities not to be ventured in a grave
quarterly. "Bright, broken Maginn," the leading spirit,
though as blind to Carlyle's real significance as deaf to
"the musical wisdom of Goethe's forty volumes," found
Goethe's "thunderwordoversetter's" "rumfustianish
(*rumfustianisches*) roly-poly growlery of style" a welcome
ingredient in his monthly brew. Carlyle after a while
received five guineas a sheet more than any other contributor. On August 31st he tells Goethe, "When I look
at the wonderful Chaos within me, full of natural Supernaturalism and all manner of antediluvian fragments;
and how the Universe is daily growing more mysterious
as well as more august, and the influences from without
more heterogeneous and perplexing, I see not well
what is to come of it all, and only conjecture from the
violence of the fermentation that something strange may

come." Something strange did come. He records in
his diary under date of Oct. 28, 1830: "Written a
strange piece on Clothes. Know not what will come of
it. I could make a kind of book, but cannot afford it."
At the end of the year he sums up, "One of the most
worthless years I have spent for a long time." It had
been disastrous from the severe illness of his wife, the
death of his sister Margaret ("caught in the great ocean
gently and as among thick clouds whereon hovered a
rainbow"), and much disappointment from the unprofit-
able investment of his intellectual capital in the "History
of German Literature." On Feb. 7th following he
notes, "I have some five pounds to front the world
with." On the 26th the whole available capital of his
and his brother Alick's households is reported as twelve-
pence in coppers. Alick's attempt to farm Craigenputtock had failed, and was to be given up at Whitsuntide. Some months earlier Jeffrey had wished to settle
an annuity of one hundred pounds upon Carlyle, a
munificent offer which could but be met by "the meek-
est, friendliest, most emphatic refusal for this and all
coming times."

Carlyle's next essay, the review in the *Edinburgh* of the
"Historic Survey of German Poetry," by William Taylor
of Norwich, is one of the most entertaining of his
performances. Erst the morning star of German literature in England, Taylor, like the morning star, had
been drowned in the light he announced. For thirty
years he had slept an Ephesian sleep. He took Kant
for a political reformer, lamented that Goethe had not
fulfilled the promise of his youth, had heard nothing of

Tieck, and a great deal too much of Kotzebue, as also did his readers. "I could but," says Carlyle to Goethe, "with such artillery as I had, batter him down into his original rubbish." Yet he could discern Taylor's personal worth. "A great-hearted, strong-minded man;" one, he might have added, whose originally lively powers had withered in a coterie. Taylor's "mild dogmatism, peaceable, incontrovertible, uttering the palpably absurd as if it were a mere truism" has been pourtrayed by an artist second to Carlyle alone in graphic power. (Borrow's "Lavengro," ch. 23).

The original sketch of "Sartor Resartus" had been extricated from Fraser's "durance" without protest on the latter's part, about January, 1831, and Carlyle set to work to expand it into a book. "A half-reckless casting of the brush, with its many frustrated colours, against the canvas." It seemed another hopeless investment of time and toil. But he could no other—

> "His own mind did like a tempest strong
> Come to him thus, and drive the weary wight along."

On August 4th, having for almost the only time in his life placed himself under a pecuniary obligation by borrowing £50 from the ever-helpful Jeffrey, he departed to seek a publisher in London. He lodged at 4, Ampton Street, Gray's Inn. "My dear," Mrs. Carlyle had said in finishing the manuscript, "this is a work of genius." [1] This was all the encouragement he had, and

---

[1] "The good Kadijah, we can fancy, listened to him with wonder, mixed with doubt; at length she answered, Yes, it was true

of all the wonders of the wonderful book none is more wonderful than its high spirits. Carlyle had indeed a well-founded conviction that his teaching fitted the time. He wrote to his wife: "The doctrine of the Phœnix," (a thought borrowed from Vico, by the way), "of Natural Supernaturalism, and the whole Clothes Philosophy (be it but well stated) is exactly what all intelligent men are wanting." But was it well stated? Fraser was so impressed by the lucidity of Carlyle's exposition that he offered to publish the book if Carlyle would give *him* a sum not exceeding £150 sterling. "I think you had better wait a little," suggested a friend. "Yes," answered Carlyle, "it is my purpose to wait till the end of eternity for it." Jeffrey commended the MS. to Murray, on the strength of the twenty-eight pages he had managed to get through himself. Murray actually accepted it, then became alarmed, and withdrew under pretext of not having been informed that the manuscript had been declined by Longman. Sartor's day was yet to break, but Carlyle had a great stroke of good fortune in his brother John's engagement, thanks to Jeffrey's recommendation, as travelling physician to Lady Clare. Expense was now stopped in that quarter, and there was a prospect of the money advanced coming back. Though denouncing the London *literati* as a body, Carlyle could not but be cheered by the interest they took in him. Hayward and Fonblanque encouraged

this that he said. One can fancy too the boundless gratitude of Mahomet; and how of all kindnesses she had done him, this, of believing the earnest struggling word he now spoke, was the greatest."—"Hero Worship," appositely quoted by Mr. Larkin.

him, his pupil Charles Buller sang his praises every-
where, Leigh Hunt showed him genuine affection; but
the great conquest was Stuart Mill, in whom Carlyle, on
the strength of his papers in the *Examiner*, had
expected to find a mystic, and who had been described
to him as "a converted utilitarian." Neither the
mysticism nor the conversion seemed so evident when
they met. "A fine, clear enthusiast, who will one day
come to something, yet to nothing poetical, I think; his
fancy is not rich; furthermore, he cannot laugh with any
compass." There was great mutual liking nevertheless,
but the perfect friendship which might have so largely
supplied the deficiencies of each never came, mainly
through Carlyle's abruptness. He lost a great opportunity; never again, except in Emerson, was he to meet
so loyal, manly, and chivalrous a soul. Mill records his
own impressions with charming modesty. "I did not
deem myself a competent judge of Carlyle. I felt that
he was a poet, and that I was not; that he was a man of
intuition, which I was not; and that as such he not
only saw many things long before me which I could only,
when they were pointed out to me, hobble after and
prove, but that it was highly probable he could see many
things which were not visible to me even after they were
pointed out." Mrs. Carlyle joined her husband in
October, to her delight and his, "wrapping my bleeding
mood with the softest of bandages," and finding for the
first time a female friend on her own intellectual level in
Sarah Austin. One stab to Carlyle's "bleeding mood"
was his estrangement from Irving, who, a man of
Patmos lost in Babylon, in the midst of human interests

and stern realities lived an absurd, apocalyptic life, taking
the Reform Bill for a vial and the riot in Coldbath
Fields for a trumpet, and heedless of Lord Melbourne's
shrewd suggestion, "Were there not to be many false
prophets about that time?" Carlyle was confounded by
the information that an old Annandale acquaintance,
one or two removes from an idiot, had actually cast out
a devil; but he was somewhat comforted by learning
that it had come back next week. One undeniable
miracle did come to pass. "Characteristics," the most
Sartor-like of the miscellaneous essays, written for the
*Edinburgh*, was accepted without demur, and published
without the alteration of a syllable. "Baddish," pronounced Carlyle, "with a certain beginning of deeper
insight." "I do not understand it," said Napier, "but
it has the stamp of genius." It is the most condensed
example of Carlyle's peculiar teaching to be found,
gaining perhaps in pith what it loses in sustained
eloquence. It calls down fire from heaven upon the
intellectual anarchy of the times, but no less powerfully
illustrates the writer's great and growing defect, his
injustice to his own age. Heroism had to retire two
centuries and put on a buff coat, that Carlyle might
receive as Oliver Cromwell what he rejected as Abraham
Lincoln. An essay on Schiller, written for *Fraser* a few
months previously, is remarkable as containing the germ
of "Hero Worship."

On January 24, 1832, Carlyle, still sojourning in
London, received tidings of the death of his father,
at the age of seventy-three. By January 29th he
had written the affecting tribute which stands first

in his "Reminiscences," fit prelude to the sorrow which alternately croons and wails through that woful book. He could not well have said more, and yet his utterance is that of one half inarticulate from grief. By April he was back at Craigenputtock, mourning a new loss in the death of Goethe, with whom he had for years exchanged letters meriting on both parts his own character of Goethe's correspondence with Schiller : "Worthy of classical days, when art was an inspired function, and the artist a priest and prophet." Carlyle is looking up to Goethe throughout, but he is also growing up to him. His loyal homage is tendered without servility, and accepted without condescension. Goethe is not only approvingly sympathetic, but practically helpful : if he sees in Carlyle rather a missionary of German culture than a self-subsisting genius, this lay in the nature of the case. But Prometheus knew that he had fire of his own ; in May, 1834, he tells Eckermann that the flame of German thought is fairly kindled in England, and that he will take his bellows and blow elsewhere. From the time of his return to Scotland he enjoyed a new resource in correspondence with Mill, who was enchanted with the review of Croker's Boswell, just published in *Fraser.* It is indeed one of Carlyle's greatest essays, written, Mrs. Carlyle told Mrs. Gilchrist, as a commission, to be ready by a fixed day. "Carlyle always writes well when he writes fast." It was but natural that he should appreciate a kindred spirit in Johnson. In rugged kindliness and intellectual massiveness, in physical tribulations and the circumstances of their struggle with the world, the two were so close a parallel that Carlyle's power of sympathetic discernment was probably never less taxed than by this noble portrait. To detect the heroic in Boswell needed insight: the piercing clearness of Carlyle's vision is best appreciated by comparison with the glowing but commonplace portrait by Macaulay. Macaulay depicts, but Carlyle reveals. Macaulay's Boswell is the Boswell of his neighbours; Carlyle's, at least in some degree, the Boswell of his Maker. His next important production, the essay on Goethe in the *Foreign Quarterly* for July, was an event in its day; if less notable now, the cause is the general acceptance of its point of view. A short article on Ebenezer Elliott's "Corn Law Rhymes," his last contribution to the *Edinburgh*, indicates the vein of thought which was to develop into "Chartism" and "Past and Present." Proposals for essays on Napoleon, Byron, Luther, were coldly received: Carlyle had plainly overdrawn his account with Napier. He found, however, occupation till October in composing an article on Diderot for the *Foreign Quarterly*, an advance in some respects upon all previous work. Never before had he manifested such faculty for wresting information from a mass of literature, and presenting a clear definite likeness of an encyclopædic personage. Voltaire's features had not been easy to mistake, but Diderot's countenance, equally Protean in its changefulness, and less characteristic in its lineaments, owes much of its impressiveness to the skill of the artist. Admirable, too, is the fearless candour with which Diderot's life and opinions are exhibited in what most would call their naked deformity; in the confidence, on the one hand, that his fidelity and his faculty will justify his biographer's kindness; on the other, that the scepticism of the Encyclopædic age needs only to be impartially set forth to be recognized as an intellectual bankruptcy, not to be coveted by any man.

In the autumn of 1832 Carlyle records that his essay on Goethe has helped him to repay Jeffrey's loan, and that the solitude of Craigenputtock has become unendurable. Not only so, but he has formed projects impossible of execution without a library. His work on Diderot had opened his mind to the significance of the French Revolution, on which he wished to write, and he hoped to find materials for his work at Edinburgh. The Carlyles accordingly repaired thither towards the end of 1832. With the literary circles of Edinburgh ("a wretched infidel place," he calls it now), he did not get on. They thought him an Orson; he acquiesced with the amendment, John the Baptist. But he found what he sought in the Advocates' Library, and was also helped by Mill, who sent him Thiers's history. The substance of his thought at the time is thus condensed in his journal—

"That the Supernatural differs not from the Natural is a great truth, which the last century (especially in France) has been engaged in demonstrating. The Philosophers went far wrong, however, in this, that instead of raising the natural to the supernatural, they strove to sink the supernatural to the natural. The gist of my whole way of thought is to do not the latter, but the former. I feel it to be the epitome of much good for this and following generations in my hands, and in those of innumerable stronger ones."

While thus slowly becoming conscious of his mission

among men, he was paying for his Edinburgh lodgings by his essay on the prince of quacks, Cagliostro—a sermon made amusing by its biographical form, whose pith may be thus conveyed—" Be a whole man. If you will not, as Goethe and I bid you, live wholly in the good, the beautiful, and the true : live wholly in the bad, the ugly, and the false. To try to live in both is to live wholly in the latter, doing the Devil's work without getting his wages." The essay, written in March, appeared in *Fraser's Magazine* for July and August ; and somewhere between these dates Fraser agreed to publish "Sartor Resartus" in the next volume, only fining Carlyle eight guineas a sheet for his originality.

Carlyle had brought from Edinburgh materials for his history of the "Diamond Necklace" that was to have been Marie Antoinette's, but the effort to string them together was for the time ineffectual. As he sat despondent one August day a carriage drove to the door and a young American alighted. It was Emerson, looking for a wise man ; the first human being, said Mrs. Carlyle, who had visited Dunscore parish on such an errand since Noah's flood. He brought letters of introduction from Gustave D'Eichthal and Stuart Mill, and had been directed on his way by Alexander Ireland, whom he had met in Edinburgh. Never since Macbeth encountered the witches had there been so memorable a meeting on a Scotch moor. Emerson had written little, but he was the same man as when he wrote "Nature" three years afterwards. Carlyle's graphic talk riveted him. "Christ died on the tree ; that built Dunscore kirk yonder." He found his host " the most simple, frank, amiable person. He worships a man that will manifest any truth to him." Emerson could hardly get as far as that : his principal teacher had been Plato, whom Carlyle " did not read." But he could and did cheer the despondent prophet by repercussion of the echoes he had awakened in America. " That," said Mrs. Carlyle, " is always the way, whatever he has written that he thinks has fallen dead he hears of two or three years afterwards." " I could not help," says Emerson, very naturally, "congratulating him upon his treasure of a wife." Carlyle on his part pronounced Emerson " one of the most lovable creatures in himself we had ever looked on." Next morning Plato's comely disciple came forth from Carlyle's furnace without the smell of fire upon him, but warmed by a glow of friendly admiration which was to have noteworthy results. Another intellectual inti-macy was already producing consequences of even greater moment. Mill's positive disinclination to undertake the history of the French Revolution, mainly prompted; there is good reason to believe, by generous considera-tion for Carlyle, decided the struggle in the latter's mind between that subject and the life of John Knox. He began by finishing the " Diamond Necklace," a master-piece of tragi-comedy in narrative, proving that he had all the power needful for the dramatic treatment of his-tory. He now longed to go to Paris and spend the winter in studying the French Revolution, but the narrowness of his means forbade. The " Diamond Necklace " was de-clined by the *Foreign Quarterly*, and a proffered essay on St. Simonianism fared no better. There was nothing to look forward to but the curtailed remuneration for "Sartor," the publication of which commenced in November. A visit from an invalid friend, William Glen, who taught him Greek in return for lessons in geometry, acquainted him in some degree with Homer. "A most quieting wholesome task too." His few remarks show that the grand simplicity of Homer was beginning to dawn upon him, and that Greek might have been an important element in his mental culture, could he have given it more time. But his circumstances allowed him no leisure to be a learner in any school but the school of adversity: he would fain have lived to teach, he must now teach to live.

Could he profess astronomy? The idea occurred to him on reading in a newspaper that a new astronomical professorship was to be established in Edinburgh. On the impulse of the moment he sat down and wrote to solicit Jeffrey's interest (Jan. 11, 1834). He had read the stars amiss, the conjuncture was most inauspicious. Jeffrey was already hoping that the appointment would be given to a former secretary of his own, better qualified than Carlyle. His estimate of Carlyle's literary power did not disincline him to help his suitor to waste his genius "by stingy star-shine," but the unjustifiableness of the request was very clear to him. Carlyle was an excellent mathematician; he could literally, as well as in Marcus Aurelius's sense, "consider the course of the stars as if he was driving through the sky with them;" he had written splendidly of "Boötes, leading his hunting-dogs over the zenith in their leash of sidereal fire." But he was unpractised in the handling of instruments, and in all probability would soon tire of the post. He would owe the appointment, if he got it, to no proof of his fitness, but

solely to the electors' respect for the Lord Advocate.
Was it right that this influence should be used to the
prejudice of a more capable man ? Jeffrey's refusal
was honourable and every way laudable; unfortunately
he could not forego the opportunity of reading Carlyle a
lecture. There existed, he said, another Professorship,
a Professorship of Rhetoric, to which he could conscien-
tiously have helped Carlyle, and to which Carlyle might
have laid strong claim, if with his perverse, foolish, pre-
posterous affectation of singularity, he had not made the
mention of his name in connection with such an office
ridiculous. It could only be conferred on some one of
established reputation, and for such a character Carlyle
had wilfully disqualified himself. It was beyond Carlyle's
power to digest this bitter melon. The pang of his self-
love was too acute for gratitude and reason. No open
estrangement ensued, but his friendship for Jeffrey was
henceforth a hollow wraith, and no words of his do him
less honour than his allusions to the transaction, whether
in his private correspondence or in his " Reminiscences."
It is but too clear that he had long chafed at Jeffrey's
kindness ; and that he was wanting in that noblest magnanimity that without sense of humiliation and with open
sunny gratitude can accept a benefit from man like a
blessing from Heaven.

One good result at least was furthered by this unfortunate business, the Carlyles' determination to " burn
their ships," abandon Craigenputtock, and make for
London. The cup ran over with the revolt of a servant-
maid, a humble instrument in the hands of Providence.
" We said to one another, ' Why not bolt out of all these

sooty despicabilities?'  Two days after we had a letter
on the road to Mrs. Austin, to look out among the houses
to let for us, and an advertisement to MacDiarmid to
try for the letting of our own."  Cattle, poultry, and
surplus furniture were sold off.  Carlyle, firmly believing
that London houses, like Edinburgh houses, could only
be taken at Whitsuntide, rushed off alone to London,
and was guided by Leigh Hunt to the house, No. 5
(afterwards 24), Cheyne Row, where he was to spend the
rest of his life.  Mrs. Carlyle soon followed; and on June
10th the family and luggage, including their invaluable
Bessy Barnet, daughter of the housekeeper of Carlyle's
Birmingham friend Badams, and the canary Chico, "were
all tumbled down."  A few days later Carlyle wrote to his
mother—

"We lie safe at a bend of the river, away from all the great
roads, have air and quiet hardly inferior to Craigenputtock, an outlook from the back windows into mere leafy regions with here and
there a red high-peaked old roof looking through ; and see nothing
of London, except by day the summits of St. Paul's Cathedral and
Westminster Abbey, and by night the gleam of the great Babylon
affronting the peaceful skies.  The house itself is probably the best
we have ever lived in—a right old, strong, roomy brick house,
built near 150 years ago, and likely to see three races of these
modern fashionables fall before it comes down."

## CHAPTER IV

" THE prosperity of a jest lies in the ear of him that hears it." It had rested with the constituents of *Fraser's Magazine* whether Carlyle should enter London with drums beating and colours flying, or steal in as unnoticed as when, ten years before, he had come in the train of the Bullers. They had unanimously turned their thumbs up. " Sartor," the publisher acquainted him, " excites universal disapprobation." Letters poured in, countermanding subscriptions until the scaregoose should be removed. Two correspondents gave instructions in a contrary sense—one was Emerson, the other Father O'Shea, a Roman Catholic priest in Cork. But priest and philosopher were no match for the multitude. A reprint was out of the question. " Sartor "—*resartus* anew—was stitched up, and circulated in pamphlet form among the fit and few—fifty, all told.

Had Carlyle's readers taken his advice to shut their Byrons and open their Goethes, they might have learned that a work of genuine art commonly displeases at first sight from the disparity between the object contemplated and the person contemplating, which irritates the latter by suggesting a deficiency in himself. To comprehend and enjoy a beautiful novelty implies the development of new power as well as the perception of new loveliness. No style, perhaps, excites in novices such instinctive recalcitrancy as Carlyle's; and "Sartor" was placed at especial disadvantage by the serial publication, which obscured the author's drift, while intervening distractions washed away any impression he might have made "like lions' footmarks from the ocean sands."

Under the quaint semblance of a Clothes Philosophy, "Sartor Resartus" teaches that Man and all things cognizable by him are but vestures of the only Reality, God. In the language of metaphysics, they are manifestations of the Absolute under the conditions of Space and Time. In Carlyle's simpler idiom,

"All visible things are emblems; what thou seest is not there on its own account; strictly taken, is not there at all : Matter exists only spiritually, and to represent some idea, and *body* it forth. On the other hand, all emblematic things are properly Clothes, thought-woven or hand-woven. Whatsoever sensibly exists, whatsoever represents Spirit to Spirit, is properly a Clothing, a suit of Raiment, put on for a season, and to be laid off. Thus in this one pregnant subject of Clothes, rightly understood, is included all that men have thought, dreamed, done and been : the whole External Universe and what it holds is but Clothing ; and the essence of all Science lies in the Philosophy of Clothes."

Who can deny the reasonableness of this on seeing so memorable a book spun from a single metaphor?—a metaphor relieved however by copious "gaseous-chaotic" autobiographical details casting a fitful light on "the perhaps unparalleled psychical mechanism" of the imaginary writer, Herr Diogenes Teufelsdröckh, Professor der Allerley-Wissenschaft at Weissnichtwo; expounding "by what singular stair-steps and subterranean passages, and Sloughs of Despair, and steep Pisgah hills, he reached this wonderful prophetic Hebron (a true Old Clothes Jewry) where he now dwells."

The germ of "Sartor" may be found in a passage of Scripture :—"As a vesture Thou shalt change them, and they shall be changed." In process of time the metaphor by which the Hebrew poet had expressed the nothingness of the material heavens in comparison with Almighty power was found equally applicable to the structure of human society. Goethe comprehends all finite existence in his description of the work of the Earth Spirit—

> " Ich sitz' an die säuselnde Webstuhl der Zeit,
> Und wirke des Gottes lebendiges Kleid."

> " Thus at the roaring loom of Time I ply,
> And weave for God the robe thou seest Him by."

Like the mythical demigods, Carlyle's "Sartor" springs from the union of an immortal father and an earthly mother. Goethe and Swift encountered in his head. The author of "A Tale of a Tub" had told us long before how philosophers "held the universe to be a suit of clothes, which invests everything. Look on this globe of earth, and you will find it to be a very complete and fashionable dress. What is that which men call land, but a fine coat faced with green? or the sea but a waistcoat of water-tabby? What is man himself but a micro-coat, or rather a complete suit of clothes with all its trimmings?"

Goethe's sublimity impregnated Swift's drollery, and
" Sartor " was their offspring, a child favouring both
parents. The double strain is mystically indicated in
the very name of the hero, Diogenes Teufelsdröckh
(Godborn Devilsdung). He has two gospels, the Clothes
Philosophy and the autobiography in the six zodiacal
bags : two apostles, an ardent Peter in Heuschrecke, a
doubting Thomas in Carlyle : two styles, which Jerrold
would have discriminated as Æschylous and Burl-
æschylous. But, above all, he has two philosophies :
he thinks as an Idealist, and feels as a Realist. " It is
his humour to look at all matter and material of things
as spirit : " to him the steamboat with all her speed and
freight of souls and noisy churning of the waters is but
the Idea of a Scotch mechanic ; but his conception of
spirit is more concrete than the materialist's conception
of matter. In painting the phantasmal unsubstantiality
of the warrior and his steed he is as real as Homer, as
vivid as Job. " That warrior on his strong war-horse,
fire flashes through his eyes ; force dwells in his arm and
heart : but warrior and war-horse are a vision, a revealed
Force, nothing more. Stately they tread the Earth, as if
it were a firm substance : fool ! the Earth is but a film,
it cracks in twain, and warrior and war-horse sink beyond
plummet's sounding. Plummet's ? Fantasy herself will
not follow them. A little while ago, they were not ; a
little while, and they are not, their very ashes are not."
This is not the Idealism that

> " Casts on all things surest, brightest, best,
> Doubt, insecurity, astonishment."

It is rather the Imagination that

> " Gives to airy nothing
> A local habitation and a name."

An idealist in a sense Carlyle certainly was, but not in the sense of those reasoners who regard all phenomena as affections of their own sentiency. He would have held with Professor Masson's typical Realist that " sweep away all existing minds [*but One*], and the deserted Earth would continue to spin round all the same, still whirling its rocks, trees, clouds, and all the rest of its material garniture, alternately in the sunshine and in the depths of the starry stillness. Though no eye should behold and no ear should hear, there would be evenings of silver moonlight on the ocean-margin, and the waves would roar as they broke and retired." His idealism is thus not the idealism of Berkeley, or the Hindu doctrine of Maya. The shows of the external world are to him indeed phantoms, but not illusions. Shadows they may be, but shadows cast by an infinite Reality. Half of the didactic portion of "Sartor Resartus" is employed in vehement assertion of this reality of the Divine Mind and the merely phenomenal character of all other existence: the other half in the most unsparing application of the principle to human creeds and institutions, which are treated as symbols, "the Godlike manifest to sense." All are for an age or ages, none are for all time.

" As Time adds much to the sacredness of Symbols, so likewise in his progress he at length defaces, or even desecrates them ; and Symbols, like all terrestrial garments, wax old. A Hierarch there-fore, and Pontiff of the World will we call him, the Poet and

inspired Maker : who, Prometheus-like, can shape new Symbols
and bring new fire from heaven to fix it there.   Such, too, will not
always be wanting : neither perhaps now are.   Meanwhile, as the
average of matters goes, we account him Legislator and wise who
can so much as tell when a Symbol has grown old, and gently remove it."

Carlyle's political writings stamp him as himself
hierarch rather than lawgiver.   It was not his mission to
legislate, but to inspire legislators.   Every man who since
his time has tried to lift politics above party has owed
something directly or indirectly to his influence, and
the best have owed the most.   But perhaps his chief
debtors are the English language and the thought of
ordinary men.   He was not, indeed, the pattern prose
writer of his day, and the aping of his peculiarities has
made many ridiculous.   But he gave what Southey and
Macaulay and Landor had not to give, he contributed
new elements instead of merely refining the old.   He
stemmed the inevitable, because indispensable, tide of
Latinism and Gallicism with a Teutonic torrent, demonstrating that word-borrowing was not yet universal,
or word-making extinct, and that the language was
not conterminous with any extant dictionary.[1]   To
the multitude of thinking men who have no relish for

[1] It is scarcely realized with what difficulty words now found
indispensable, both exotic and Anglo-Saxon, established themselves,
or regained their ancient acceptance.   Emerson, even in a private
letter, only ventures on *potentially* with the apology, "as Mr.
Coleridge would say."   John Edward Taylor, writing in 1830,
underlines *nescience* with deprecatory italic.   James Grant scruples
at *uncouth*.

abstractions he brought thoughts in the guise of things. His arguments as well as his illustrations are commonly couched in metaphor. He thus captivates the poetical and imaginative mind, so inaccessible to dry reasoning. They, for example, whom the proposition " that all things are a perpetual flux" leaves as cold as it found them, will kindle at hearing from Carlyle that " the drop which thou shakest from thy wet hand rests not where it falls, but to-morrow thou findest it swept away: already, on the wings of the North wind, it is nearing the Tropic of Cancer." While familiar circumstances are thus gorgeously embellished, a philosophy is sometimes condensed into a phrase. Whatever, for instance, Darwin and Spencer and Samuel Butler can tell us of the influence of hereditary descent, is divined and prophetically depicted by Carlyle in a sentence: " Noteworthy also, and serviceable for the progress of this same Individual, wilt thou find his subdivision into Generations."

While still-born "Sartor" lay lifeless in men's sight like the bodies of the witnesses awaiting the resurrection, Carlyle was addressing himself to the history of the French Revolution. " I write my book," he said, "without hope of it, except of being done with it." His sole encouragement was the assurance that it would not need to be published at his own expense. Profit he hardly dared hope for : and unless he could stoop to be a burden to his mother-in-law, it was not apparent what he would have to live upon when the proceeds of the Craigenputtock sale should be exhausted. His mind was further anguished by the pathetic death of Irving (Dec. 1834).

Excluded from his own Church really for his eccentricities, but ostensibly for what Carlyle thought a saving grain of good sense, Irving had founded a church of his own, and at least proved his sincere faith in the revival of the Pentecostal gift by laying no claim to possess it himself. Authority consequently passed from him to the more highly favoured, who used it to break his heart. Carlyle's lamentation is touching : like the prophet of old he cries, "Alas, my brother!" He seems to reproach himself with having omitted "sweeping in upon all tongue work and accursed choking cobwebberies, and snatching away my old best friend, to save him from death and the grave." But surely without cause. Irving's doom was sealed on the day when he made up his mind that the world would not last his time. Could he have believed by halves, all secular things might have gone well with him.

Carlyle's trials plead ample excuse for much unreasonableness : even his injustice might have passed unnoticed if it had not lived after him by the indiscretion of his editor and biographer. He chose to think himself ill-treated because he was not offered the editorship of the new *London and Westminster Review ;* as if the earnest and munificent man who founded it ought to have lavished his money to propagate Carlyle's ideas, instead of his own. "A poorish narrow creature," says the disappointed candidate for the editorship. "I have known no man," says Chorley, "as regards heart, head, and capacity, superior to Sir William Molesworth." Carlyle's "Reminiscences" should never be printed without this antidote, and would be profited by the like commentary throughout. Carlyle expected that the editorship would be bestowed on W. J. Fox, a safer man and a better Liberal, utilitarian by conviction, poetical by temperament, the first rhetorician of his time, and not the last orator. It was, however, eventually undertaken by Mill himself: if he really manifested any embarrassment on announcing that Carlyle was not to have it, it can only have been from surprise that such an announcement should be needful. In the midst of his grumbling, Carlyle's truthfulness comes finely out. "Mill," he says, "was very useful about French Revolution; lent me all his books, which were quite a collection on that subject; gave me frankly, clearly, and with zeal, all his better knowledge than my own, being full of eagerness for such an advocate in that cause as he felt I should be. Talk rather wintry ('sawdustish,' as old Sterling once called it), but always well informed and sincere." Of Mill's Egeria, Mrs. Taylor, we obtain some glimpses. She is "pale and passionate and sad-looking, a living romance heroine, of the royallest volition and questionable destiny;" also "iridescent" and "veevid," epithets rather suggestive than definite. Mrs. Carlyle writes that she might be her friend, but is deemed dangerous; while from Carlyle we gather that she was worse than dangerous, she was patronizing. On the whole Mill's fine essay on Tennyson, revealing a new order of thought with him, remains the best evidence of the light and leading he was undoubtedly receiving from her.

Mill and Mrs. Taylor between them were to purge Carlyle's soul by pity and terror. The first volume of the "French Revolution," now ready in manuscript, had been

lent to Mill, who, probably without leave asked, had lent
it to Mrs. Taylor.   On the evening of March 6, 1835,
Mill, "distraction in his aspect," rushed into Carlyle's
parlour, and entreated Mrs. Carlyle to go and speak to a
lady sitting in a carriage at the door.   "Something dread-
ful has happened, she'll tell you what."   Mrs. Carlyle
sprang into the carriage, but the lady would only say,
"Oh! you'll never speak to him again!"   Mrs. Carlyle
sped back to the gentlemen, and saw Carlyle emblem-
atically rolling up a paper match.   "Tell me what has
happened!"   "What? hasn't she told you? Your
husband's manuscript is entirely destroyed!"   It had,
indeed, been burned ; by the negligence of Mrs. Taylor's
servant.   Mrs. Taylor drove away.   Mill, deceived by
Carlyle's stoicism, or thinking to cheer him, maintained
for two hours a lugubrious attempt at conversation.   He
went away at last "in a relapsed state, one of the piti-
ablest."   When left alone with his wife, Carlyle's first
words were, "Well, Mill, poor fellow, is terribly cut up;
we must endeavour to hide from him how very serious
the business is to us."   Serious indeed.   The book had
been Carlyle's "last throw."   Composition was to him a
terrible intellectual travail.   He had kept no notes, and
could not recall a sentence that he had written.   He
shrank with quivering nerves from the task of recon-
struction, which must be faced nevertheless.   Day after
day he recoiled beaten.   After two months' fruitless
struggle he has to tell Emerson, "I with a new effort
of self-denial sealed up all the paper fragments, and said
to myself: 'In this mood thou makest no way, writest
nothing that requires not to be erased again : lay it by

for one complete week.'" "Such mischance," wrote
Emerson, "might well quicken one's curiosity to know
what Oversight there is of us." "My belief in a special
Providence grows yearly stronger, unsubduable, impreg-
nable," wrote Carlyle. Providence did indeed visibly
interpose, not by inspiring Mill to make atonement as far
as money could, which was a matter of course with him,
but by disposing Carlyle to receive half the two hundred
pounds pressed on his acceptance. To have refused
would have been cruelty to Mill and injustice to himself,
but never before had he been so reasonable. He made
his pride some amends by declining Mill's generous offer
to publish the "Diamond Necklace" at his own expense,
"that he might have the pleasure of reviewing it."

Another rejection of proffered benefit about this time
does Carlyle high honour. Mill—ever his good angel
except in the matter of the burnt manuscript—had sent
him while he yet dwelt in Scotland an anonymous novel
entitled "Arthur Coningsby," which impressed Carlyle
as the production of "an opulent, genial, and sunny mind,
but misdirected, disappointed, experienced in misery."
This chiaroscuro soul inhabited the mortality of John
Sterling, one of the young disciples of Coleridge who had
modified, without subverting, Mill's utilitarian creed.
Carlyle, already well inclined to him, made his acquaintance in February, 1835, and noticed "the kindly but
restless swift-glancing eyes, which looked as if the spirits
were all out coursing like a pack of merry beagles, beating
every bush." Sterling had just resigned his curacy under
Julius Hare at Hurstmonceaux from ill health, but was still
ecclesiastical in garb and heart. It struck him at once that

if what Shelley had called "certain technicalities" when *he* thought of taking orders admitted of adjustment, Carlyle would make a model clergyman: whether he discerned the promise and the potency of episcopacy in him we do not know. By way of a beginning he introduced him to his father, Edward Sterling, the leading writer, though not the leading mind, of *The Times*. The result was an offer of employment on the journal: a position for which no man is too able, and but few are too independent. Carlyle was one of the latter, he nobly refused, feeling that he could place himself at the service of no political party without violence to his conscience. "Radicalism," he wrote to Emerson, "I feel to be a wretched necessity, unfit for me; Conservatism being not unfit only, but false for me; yet these two are the grand categories under which all English spiritual activity that so much as thinks remuneration possible must range itself." On similar and other no less cogent grounds he declined an editorship at Lichfield, where an infant was being reared to write his biography. A kindly meant but maladroit offer of a clerkship from Basil Montagu exploded a long-accumulating magazine of wrath. Mrs. Carlyle had never forgiven Mrs. Montagu for her officious interference with her affairs, and Carlyle was more under his wife's influence than he knew. Fraser was still obdurate, hoping, Carlyle darkly surmised, to get the "Diamond Necklace" for nothing. Mill could offer him no work on the *London and Westminster* for awe of his stern father, who thought Carlyle an insane rhapsodist, and whose health required great forbearance. There was nothing to be done but to pound steadily at the "French Revolution." Relieved by the mental opiate of a course of Marryat's novels, Carlyle resumed his pen. While straining after the fancied perfection of the first draught he received admonition from a bricklayer, as Robert Bruce had from a spider. Watching the man at his work, " the busy trowel running to and fro and flashing in the light like a swallow," he noticed that he gave himself little trouble to make his lines rigorously straight, but seemed mainly intent on getting his house built. " I came to the conclusion that striving after perfection beyond a certain degree was simply foolish, and I was thus encouraged to write the volume again as best I could." So vigorously did he proceed that the annihilated chapters were recreated by Sept. 22nd. " I do not think," writes Mrs. Carlyle, " that the new version is on the whole inferior to the first ; it is a little less vivacious, perhaps, but better thought and put together." " It never seemed to Carlyle so good as the first copy, and yet he could not remember what the first was."

Carlyle toiled at his history during 1836, "mind weary, body very sick, little black specks dancing to and fro in the left eye." His labour was only interrupted to trim a detached splinter struck off at his work —the essay on Mirabeau, shaped and polished for the *London and Westminster* "at the passionate request of Stuart Mill," whose father had died in June, "and likewise for needful lucre." Ill-health drove Mrs. Carlyle to her mother in the summer ; and in the autumn John Sterling, under the like compulsion, sought the South of France. He had wound himself round Carlyle's heart. " I love him better," he says to Emerson, " than anybody I have met with since a certain sky-messenger

alighted to me at Craigenputtock and vanished in the
blue again." His portrait of Sterling as he appeared at
this time, though the artist has no notion of it, is strikingly
like Shelley. Sterling, on his part, introduced Carlyle
into his " Onyx Ring," painting him as he delved in his
little garden, and telling how his phrases kept ringing in
one's ears days and nights after utterance, as if he had
sent a goblin trumpeter to haunt one with the sound.
Leigh Hunt, also, a near neighbour, contributed not a
little to brighten Carlyle's life. His domestic arrangements filled the latter with wondering disapproval, and
pity for the sickly wife asleep on cushions and the four
or five beautiful, strange, gipsy-looking children running
about in undress. (" Without parallel even in literature.
An indescribable dream-like household.") But Hunt
received visitors like a king, apologizing for nothing ;
and when, leaving his cares behind him, he came as a
guest, he charmed by his sincerity and cordiality, set off
by the " aërial politeness " which made him a partaker
of the Carlyles' oatmeal porridge, " in a tiny basin," adds
Carlyle with delicious simplicity. Carlyle thought Hunt
fantastic and idly melodious ; but nothing better than his
description, even when he scolds, proclaims the sterling
worth and sprightly valour of the man. " I believe,"
wrote Hunt, possibly thinking of himself, " that what Mr.
Carlyle loves better than his fault-finding, with all its
eloquence, is the face of any human creature that looks
suffering and loving and sincere." Best of all was the
proof afforded by an American edition of " Sartor " that
the " high-flaming pitch-pan, kindled in a lonely watch-
tower," had shot a beam across the Atlantic. Emerson
had been the only American subscriber, or at least

possessed the only accessible copy. This he gave to his betrothed, and it became known in her circle. Two intimates, Dr. Le Baron Russell and William Silsbee, unable to beg, borrow, or steal, resolved to reprint. After a while Messrs. Munroe relieved them of the responsibility, Emerson wrote a preface, and the book was published in an edition of five hundred copies, April, 1836. Carlyle slyly quotes it in his essay on Mirabeau as the work of a New England author. Another edition was soon required. Even in England it began to creep into notice, although, as Mrs. Carlyle remarked, "only completely understood and adequately appreciated by women and mad people. I do not know very well what to infer from the fact."

"Mirabeau" and "The Diamond Necklace," the latter tardily victorious over Fraser's coyness, were before the world ere, on January 12, 1837, Carlyle wrote the last word of "The French Revolution" as the clock was striking ten and the supper of oatmeal porridge was coming up. He naturally felt the house too narrow, and went forth into the night. Before departing he said to his wife, "I know not whether this book is worth anything, nor what the world will do with it, or misdo, or entirely forbear to do, as is likeliest: but this I could tell the world: You have not had for a hundred years any book that comes more direct and flamingly from the heart of a living man. Do what you like with it, you." After which oration, the hall-door closed upon the most angry and desperate man of genius then in the flesh; with cause, had he known it, to have been the most thankful and hopeful.

## CHAPTER V

" OUR young men," Emerson told Carlyle, "say yours is the only history they have ever read." It was the only *such* history they or any one had at that time ever read. Its manner was not unknown in memoirs, in novels, in books of travel, even in detached passages and paragraphs of histories ; but no complete history on its plan yet existed in the world. To give Carlyle's method the briefest possible definition, were perhaps to say that he strove to write history in the study as he would have reported it in the street. He relied upon personal memoirs, to a degree unusual even in a historian of France. While other historians had sought to blend these details into a smooth equable narrative, as rags are fashioned into a sheet of paper, Carlyle took the rags themselves and hung them forth gay or grimy or blood-stained, dancing in air or trailing in mud. Other historians gave the Revolution at second-hand, but he at first-hand. That peculiar feeling of reality, as if one's own blood bounded with the emotion of the event, which others have successfully called up in detached scenes, as Schiller in his description of the battle of Lutzen, Carlyle excited throughout a long history. The secret was his power of such thorough identification with the feelings of the actors in the occurrences that the reader felt a hearer, and the hearer felt a witness, and the witness seemed well-nigh an actor in the impassioned drama.

This power was not peculiar to Carlyle, it belongs more or less to all poets and novelists who excel in the delineation of action. He had, however, a great advantage over most poets and novelists in his intense penetration with his subject. He wrote less as an artist than as a prophet. He believed that the French Revolution was the living manifestation of the truths he held most dear. The sublimity of fact, the impotence of phrase, the folly of formula, the loathsomeness of rotten institutions, the reeling frenzy of the unguided multitude, the saving virtue of efficiency, that salt of scoundrelism; these things he saw written throughout the whole eventful history. He need not, as in "Sartor," spin his argument from his own brain, the facts would preach eloquently enough. He was fortunate moreover in a subject which exactly fitted his style. Vividness is always a precious quality, yet some incongruity must have been felt if the tale of ancient Greece or modern Italy had been told in the language of the "French Revolution." Nor could such a style have been proper or even practicable where the element of first-hand testimony was less pre-ponderating. But the French Revolution was volcanic enough to justify Carlylean vehemence of treatment; and its archives, whether extant in contemporary pamphlets or in memoirs, were the work of those who spoke of what they knew and testified of what they had seen.

Many objections may be made to Carlyle's history.

Some may be dismissed by Mill's general answer that genius is a law unto itself. Other defects, though real, are sufficiently excused by the circumstances of the author, and the deficiency of the information to which he had access. It may be that the abuses of the old *régime* were not so monstrous, or the condition of the people so miserable, or the uprising of "disimprisoned anarchy" so inevitable as he thought: but if so this only weakens one half of his case to fortify the other, for the governing classes must have been even more corrupt and incapable. Writing at a period of tranquillity, he not unnaturally underestimated the vitality of "Sans-culottism" and made too much of the "whiff of grape-shot" which was rather an incident in the drama than its catastrophe. For this he partly made amends in the sixth lecture of his "Hero Worship." A more serious defect is his partiality. He sees his personages as incarnations of his own admirations and aversions, and treats them accordingly. He caresses his blackguards of genius, Mirabeau and Danton, men of a type common in every stormy period; and persistently runs down Robespierre, the incarnation of the ideas of the Revolution, whose intellect, he afterwards admitted to Professor Masson, he felt that he had underrated. He does not make nearly sufficient account of the baleful part played by Marie Antoinette. At the same time, nothing can be more living than his portraits; the error, when error there is, is not in painting, but in grouping. Memory will not soon part with "the sea-green incorruptible;" "swart, burly-headed Mira-beau;" "Scipio Americanus" Lafayette; the "large-headed dwarfish individual, of smoke-bleared aspect," who died by the hand of Charlotte Corday. His stereoscopic imagination, to use Emerson's happy phrase, not only makes the object visible, but detaches it from the background. The pictures on a large scale are not less admirable than the portraits, though their apparent breadth resolves itself on examination into the combined effect of an infinity of sharp incisive strokes. Such are the swarm of picturesque items that tell with a thousand tongues the tale of the taking of the Bastille; and the long-drawn agony of the royal flight to Varennes, where every weary wasted minute seems charmed back with all its misery from the gulf of the Past.

It may be questioned how far Carlyle is entitled to the character of a philosophic historian. In one sense he has certainly little claim to the title, for his point of view fluctuates between earth and heaven. "The French Revolution" is to him a manifestation of the Supreme: at the same time it is an exhibition of individual character in its most intense form. The former thought, logically carried out, would have led him to fatalism; but the freedom of the will was the very battle-ground on which he had defeated the Everlasting No. The other would have conducted him to a denial of Providential agency, the strongest conviction he held. He seems to dwell alternately in one or other of these views as his humour prompts, or as the exigencies of his narrative require. But if it be philosophy to have a hold on first principles, few historians have been so truly philosophical. His principles are very few but very sufficient, and might, but for the dignity of history, be expressed in half-a-dozen of the homeliest proverbs current among men. The noblest philosophical explanation of the Revolution he did not, could not attempt. Every event becomes clear when fully viewed in all its antecedents and all its consequences. To grasp the first would require more erudition than Carlyle had, more than a man of his original power ought to have ;—and the creature of a day cannot await Time's deliberate unfolding of the Past.

The " French Revolution " has been more popular in England than most of Carlyle's books. Its direct and indirect effect on the language has been great and on the whole beneficial. The small fry of imitators die off, and the traces of its influence on Dickens, Ruskin, and Browning remain. Even Macaulay owed it a debt, which he had no mind to pay. It is still mainly a possession of the English-speaking peoples. M. Taine's well-known criticism sums up the difficulties of French readers. There is a good French translation by Regnault and Barot. The translators justly indicate Michelet's resemblance to Carlyle, which is indeed remarkable. They then, ignorant or oblivious or contemptuous of Shakespeare and Milton, label him in the neat French manner as *le phénomène d'un protestant poétique* (!) One of the highest compliments he received from a foreign critic came from Prosper Mérimée, who, in a letter written while reading him, described his almost irresistible inclination to pitch him out of the window. Mérimée, a man made for better things, had cast in his lot with the Third Empire ; and must have felt as Felix felt when Paul reasoned of the judgment to come.

Worn out by his book and his lectures, of which presently, Carlyle fled in June, 1837, to Scotsbrig, where his brother James was farming for his aged mother, and Alexander was established in a small shop. There he spent three idle months among his own clan, slightly disturbed by the inconsiderateness of a London acquaintance, who sent him the *Athenæum's* opinion of his book. But he boiled his tea-kettle with it, and peace of mind, returned. He could not complain of the general reception of the work. Mill had disarmed and intimidated commonplace criticism by a review which, though far from the best of his essays, he justly reckoned among his *Thaten in Wörten.* It put the book on the right footing from the first, pronouncing it an epic poem, which did for history whatever could be done by the best historical drama. Mill, whose own diction was so chaste and limpid, boldly declared Carlyle's style to be of surpassing excellence, a most suitable and glorious vesture for his thought. The transcendentalism with which his own philosophical creed forbade him to sympathise sprang in Carlyle from feelings the most solemn and the most deeply rooted which can lie in the heart of a human being. Jeffrey, with honourable candour, admitted the falsification of his predictions that Carlyle would commit literary suicide. Thackeray reviewed him in the *Times,* lauding his substance but lamenting his style. "Everybody is astonished at every other body's being pleased with this wonderful performance." Cash, nevertheless, was not forthcoming, could not be till the expense of publication had been paid.

Before Carlyle's flight to Scotland he had been brought into personal relations with many of the most gifted men and women in London, a great help to his eventual

success. He was largely indebted for this to Harriet
Martineau, a childless woman with a motherly heart, and
one of his most valuable friends, grievously as she bored
him with her singular experiences. ("She had once met
a man who seemed not fully convinced of the immortality
of the soul.") As early as November, 1834, Emerson
had suggested that Carlyle might lecture in America.
Miss Martineau, just returned from the United States,
where she had found lecturers a thriving species, conceived
the happy idea that he might lecture at home. With the aid
of Miss Wilson ("distinctly the cleverest woman I know,"
says Mrs. Carlyle), she set to work to carry it out. "Was
it for this," Carlyle may have thought, "that I forswore
the pulpit?" But reason pleaded on one side, shyness
only on the other; and on May 1, 1837, the day on which
Mr. Browning's "Strafford" was produced by Macready,
Hallam led him to the rostrum at Willis's Rooms, front-
ing "a crowded yet select audience of both sexes,"
gathered to hear a course of six lectures on German
Literature. There he stood, a spare figure, lacking one
inch of six feet; long but compact of head, which
seemed smaller than it really was; rugged of feature;
brow abrupt like a low cliff, craggy over eyes deep-set,
large, piercing, between blue and dark-gray, full of
rolling fire; firm but flexible lips, noway ungenial;
dark, short, thick hair, not crisp, but wavy as rock-
rooted, tide-swayed weed; complexion bilious-ruddy or
ruddy-bilious, according as Devil or Baker might be
prevailing with him. When he began the former was
decidedly in the ascendant. "I pitied myself, so agitated,
terrified, driven desperate and furious." But the *Times,*

probably with Edward Sterling's eyes, discerned "incidental streaks of light from a vivid and fine imagination," and recognized in the lecturer "a genius fitted to grapple with difficulties, and to handle vigorously materials unwieldy and intractable." The course was a great success, and produced one hundred and thirty-five pounds. The public, as Mrs. Carlyle put it, had decided that Carlyle was worth keeping alive at a moderate rate. Three more courses followed in successive years—on the History of Literature and the Periods of European Culture (twelve lectures); on the Revolutions of Modern Europe; and on Hero Worship (six lectures each). The last is known to all; the second and third were imperfectly reported in the *Examiner* by Leigh Hunt, who is always forgetting the reporter in the critic. Extracts from a full, though sometimes blundering, report of eleven lectures of the second course have been published by Professor Dowden in the *Nineteenth Century*, and are of great interest as presenting Carlyle's opinions on a number of topics not elsewhere treated by him.

Many observers have recorded their impressions of Carlyle as a lecturer. "Yellow as a guinea," says Harriet Martineau, "with downcast eyes, broken speech at the beginning, and fingers which nervously picked at the desk before him, he could not for a moment be supposed to enjoy his own effort." Ticknor saw in him "a rather small, spare, ugly Scotchman, with a strong accent." (Carlyle's beauty is a matter of opinion, but his height was five feet eleven.) To Sumner he "seemed like an inspired boy: truths and thoughts that made one move on the benches came from his apparently unconscious mind, couched in the most grotesque style, and yet condensed to a degree of intensity." Caroline Fox says: "His manner is very quiet, but he speaks like one tremendously convinced of what he utters, and who has much in him that is unutterable." These various glimpses are in general authenticated by a professional observer, James Grant, a man prejudiced neither for the lecturer nor against him, and much too prosaic to have discovered expression in Carlyle's "dark, clear, penetrating eye," or "wrapt attention" in his audience, if they had not actually been there. Grant gravely inquires whether the peculiarities of Carlyle's style were or were not to be ascribed to his having passed several years of his life in Germany, the fact itself being indubitable. "So great was the friendship which Goethe entertained for him, and so fond was he of his society, that, as he could not always be in his company, he caused a bust of him to be executed by a first-rate artist, and to be placed in his own study; in order that Mr. Carlyle's image might be constantly present to his mind." A myth whose genesis we should be glad to learn. Did it spring out of the presentation of a seal to Goethe by his English admirers? Carlyle's admirers had expected him to lecture every year, but he never liked the "mixture of prophecy and play-acting," and he was only reconciled to the mental effort by the reflection that "one must work either with long moderate pain or else with short great pain." At last the pain became too great. "It is one of the saddest conditions of this enterprise to feel that you have missed what you meant to say; that your image of a matter you had an image of remains yet with yourself, and a false impotent scrawl is what the hearers have got from you." In concluding the course on "Hero Worship" he took leave of the platform with these graceful words : "Often enough, with these abrupt utterances thrown out isolated, unexplained, has your tolerance been put to the trial. Tolerance, patient candour, all-hoping favour and kindness, of which I will not now speak. The accomplished and distinguished, the beautiful, the wise, something of what is best in England, have listened patiently to my rude words. With many feelings, I heartily thank you all, and say, Good be with you all ! "

Carlyle was now a duly certificated lion, with social opportunities which he did not put to full use. There is a discouraging want of geniality in his relations with the most eminent of his contemporaries who were personally known to him. Entries in his diary show that he was fully conscious how much better his affirmative was than his negative ; but Goethe himself had never been able to teach him the unprofitableness of continually repeating that evil is evil. Mrs. Carlyle could have helped him if she had not been a duplicate of him in this respect. Sterling's volatility sometimes provoked displeasure. "He has the mind of a kangaroo!" We must lament without wonder that he should have come to look upon Mill as "a friend frozen in ice for me." Harriet Martineau was benevolent, loyal, and practical ; but the creature had been made subject unto vanity. Landor, who himself confessed that he had done no wise things, though he had written many, Carlyle pronounced "a soul ever splashing web-footed in the terrene mud." His want of Greek culture disabled him from recognizing Landor's immortal part; yet he looked more kindly on the veteran as he drew nearer to the grave, finding in him scholarship, in the old and beautiful sense, such as he had met with in no other man. It is more surprising that he should have judged Wordsworth's poetry so ill. Due reverence for its diviner elements would have checked his contemptuous impatience of the bard's "garrulities and even platitudes" in conversation. By and by it was discovered that though Wordsworth was weak on the subject of poetry, he was great in reminiscence, and could describe persons he had known nearly as well as Carlyle's own father. "Not great, but genuine," ran the ultimate verdict. Southey suited Carlyle much better. With his piercing physiognomical observation he at once detected the fallacy of the too general estimate of Southey as a mere formalist, "starched before he was washed." "He is the most excitable, but the most methodic man I have ever seen." To his great surprise, he found Southey "full of sympathy, assent, and recognition" for his "French Revolution." "Here was a conscript father voting in a very pregnant manner." Other links of sympathy shortly appeared. Both were prophets of evil; Carlyle vehement, Southey plaintive. Elijah compared notes with Jeremiah, and their conversation surpassed anything in Nightmare Abbey. "Topic steady approach of democracy, with revolution (probably explosive) and a finis incomputable to man; steady decay of all morality, political, social, individual; this once noble England getting more and more ignoble and untrue in every fibre of it, till the gold would all be eaten out, and noble England would have to collapse in shapeless ruin, whether for ever or not none of us could know." " I remember the dialogue," says Carlyle, "as copious and pleasant (!)" When Southey was again heard of, it was to be likened to "one of those huge sandstone cylinders which I had seen at Manchester turning with inconceivable velocity till comes a moment when the stone's cohesion is quite worn out, and while grinding its fastest it flies off altogether, and settles some yards from you, a grinding-stone no longer, but a cart-load of quiet sand."

One entirely delightful episode in Carlyle's life at this time was the success of his cause in the neglected English author's high court of appeal, America. He found the truth of his own words in his first letter to Emerson : " We and you are not two countries, and cannot for the life of us be, but only two parishes of one country." A second edition of " Sartor " had already been printed, and by September, 1837, eleven hundred and sixty-six copies were sold. Some one suggested to Emerson that the author might have gained by publishing without the intervention of a bookseller, and Emerson, enchanted at the thought of being Carlyle's banker and attorney, acted on the hint, courageously taking the risk upon himself. He had to look after all arrangements. "I will," he vowed, "summon to the bargain all the Yankee in my constitution, and multiply and divide like a lion." Fifty pounds profit crossed the Atlantic bound for Carlyle in June, 1838; a hundred pounds followed in January, 1839. Meanwhile Emerson, practical as he was ardent and dis-interested, seized the idea of collecting Carlyle's miscel-laneous essays. Carlyle was to have a dollar on every

copy sold, and the entire profit upon every copy sub-
scribed for.   He was further enabled to import a number
of copies to be sold by Fraser, whom, preferring the
devil he knew to the devil he did not know, he selected
amid competing publishers.   The Miscellanies, appearing
in America in company with a financial crash, did not at
first prosper so well as Carlyle's other writings.   " My
hope," wrote Emerson, " is that you may live until this
creeping bookseller's balance shall incline at last to your
side."   Carlyle characteristically packed the account into
his drawer, " never to be looked at more except from the
outside, as a memorial of one of the best and helpfullest
of men."   The transaction is also memorable as the first
considerable instance of American insight and wisdom
in reprinting the scattered productions of a great English
author neglected by his countrymen, and as a seasonable
hint to English authors at home.   Before long Jeffrey,
Sydney Smith, and Macaulay were all reprinting.   Some
prejudice seems to have existed against essays originally
published in periodicals.   It amuses now to find even
Clough scrupling whether he could properly present
Carlyle's Miscellanies to a particular friend : "I should
not like to give him anything ephemeral."   The correspondence, though in its first period turning so much on
business matters, is as delightful from the pure disinterestedness of both writers as Goethe and Schiller's.   It
is inevitably much poorer in reflection and criticism, being
so inconsecutive and casual in comparison.   We have
luminous jets of thought, but no continuous flow.   As
a study of character, however, it is of hardly inferior
interest.   Carlyle's self-revelation is rarely more complete.

Emerson appears throughout in the fairest light, inexhaustible in graciousness and generosity, courteously deferential, but pitting his depth against his friend's strength, and most resolute where he seems most yielding. There is not a word in his share of the correspondence better unwritten, there are far too many in Carlyle's. Still we cannot but see in the ragged oak a finer object than in the shapely cypress, and with more shelter for man and beast. Emerson is not unconscious of Carlyle's intenser vitality, and receives thankfully " these stringent epistles of bark and steel and mellow wine." In return he offers, by Carlyle's own acknowledgment, the example of "a soul peaceably irrefragable in this loud-jangling world." Carlyle recognizes the peculiar qualities of Emerson's style, which he defines with inimitable felicity as "brevity, simplicity, softness, homely grace, with such a penetrating meaning, soft enough, but irresistible, going down to the depths and up to the heights, as silent electricity goes."

Carlyle's lectures enabled him to forbear from authorship until conscious of an effectual call. He had, however, promised Mill to review Lockhart's "Life of Scott," a task accomplished *invitissima Minerva* (Jan., 1838). The essay, nevertheless, is delightfully written, but breaks his master Goethe's first commandment: it is almost wholly negative, and therefore almost wholly barren. Carlyle almost seems to have conceived a grudge against Scott as he contrasted his instantaneous triumph with the neglect of Burns. He rails at Scott for possessing those business aptitudes the lack of which he deplores in others he makes him a mere speculator in literature, and will

not see that if Abbotsford was folly, it was enthusiasm.
His judgment of the Waverley Novels is singularly in-
consistent : he describes them as only good for amusing
indolence and languor, and adds that they have taught
" this truth, as good as unknown to writers of history and
others till so taught, that the byegone ages of the world
were actually filled by living men." How could he
represent this as "an achievement not of the sublime
sort, or extremely edifying"? He was more at home in
tearing to shreds in *Fraser's Magazine* (July, 1839) Barère's
great historical lie of the refusal to strike, farewell broadside, and triumphant engulphment of the crew of the *Vengeur*. " A majestic piece of *blague*, hung out dexterously,
like the Earth itself, on Nothing." "Sartor" and the Miscellanies had already appeared in English editions, and
Carlyle had been meditating an essay on Oliver Cromwell.
Mill, who had proposed the subject to him, had gone
abroad in bad health, leaving the review in charge of the
sub-editor, Robertson ("a rude Aberdeen Long-ear, full
of laughter, vanity, pepticity, and hope ; a great admirer
of mine too"). Carlyle was just about to begin writing when
Robertson considerately informed him that he need not
trouble, for "he meant to do Cromwell himself," and he
did him ; in a very good article of its kind. Carlyle
forthwith determined to write a book instead, and began
to collect materials. Another task, however, seemed
more urgent. 1838 and 1839 had been remarkable for
the growth of a new political movement, Chartism. The
Reform Bill and its train of salutary enactments had
not clothed or fed the people : or any good they might
have done in this respect had been counteracted by bad
harvests and commercial catastrophes. It was naturally

assumed that they had not been sufficiently radical, and a cry arose for universal suffrage and the other five points of the "People's Charter"; while, on the other hand, the middle classes were slipping back into Conservatism. Carlyle utterly disbelieved in the efficacy of the political reform to which the Liberals were committed, and thought that the Conservatives might carry the country with them if they would take up social reform in its place. After some unsuccessful negotiation with Mill, who was himself about to treat the subject from a different point of view, he went boldly over to Lockhart, editor of the *Quarterly*, who encouraged him to attempt an article. The result was his "Chartism," which Lockhart could but decline as ill-sorted with his review and dismaying to his party. He probably convinced Carlyle that he was not himself dismayed, for the one result of their conference was an abiding mutual regard. Mill, about to abandon the *London and Westminster*, was now anxious to print "Chartism"; he would fain have sunk with a broadside and a cheer, like the fabulous heroes of the *Vengeur*. Carlyle should have consented. But for Mill the "French Revolution" might not have been written. He had shortened its quarantine by many years : he had just found sixty-eight pages for a diffuse panegyric upon Carlyle's writings in general from the pen of Sterling. But Carlyle allowed his wife and brother to persuade him to think only of the interests of his work, which were certainly better consulted by the pamphlet form in which it was published at the end of the year. A thousand copies were sold : so high had Carlyle climbed since "Sartor."

A little book, but a great one. Wildly declamatory, truth without soberness, it contains some of Carlyle's finest writing, and is as fresh to-day as the day it was published; nor is it intolerant like its more modern representatives. It would have been easy to have annihilated the factory system upon paper. Carlyle saw that the Mersey and the collieries and the air soft with Atlantic moisture were divine injunctions to Lancashire to spin cotton. The splendid passage on Manchester proves that when he denounced the mechanism of the age, he did not mean its machinery. "There is not a bigger baby born of Time in these late centuries," he says, urging John Chorley to write the history of Lancashire. He only demanded just gains, reasonable hours of work, comfortable dwellings, pure waters, smokeless altars of industry. The main thought of his book is the denunciation of democracy as "a self-cancelling business," leading infallibly to despotism in the absence of the blessed alternative of government by Aristocracy, defined as "a corporation of the best and bravest." He had been deeply impressed in his youth by the devotion of the Scotch people to Burns. "The very inn-windows," he told Goethe, "where he had been used to scribble in idle hours with his versifying and often satirical diamond, have all been unglassed, and the scribbled panes sold into distant quarters, there to be hung up in frames." Hence he inferred that "it is the nature of men, in every time, to honour and love their Best, to know no limits to honouring them." For his ideal corporation he provides sufficient work by his demands for national instruction and systematized emigration. If this practical outcome of such passionate eloquence seems meagre, let it be remembered that education was not organized until thirty-one years afterwards, and that emigration is not organized to this day. The unpractical part of his teaching was of high value as a stimulus : he could give no test by which the aristocracy of worth might be known, and suggest no means of installing it when it was known: but many seekers found it in themselves. It was not his fault if his doctrines sometimes served the purposes of adventurers, like the French Imperial pretender he met about this time. " I sat next him at dinner and he tried to convert me to his notions, but such ideas as he possessed had no real fire in them, not so much as a capacity for flame ; his mind was a kind of extinct sulphur-pit, and gave out nothing but a smell of rotten sulphur."

## CHAPTER VI

IN "Chartism" Carlyle had called for government by a sacred band of the best and bravest. In his lectures on Hero Worship (a phrase borrowed from David Hume), delivered in May, 1840, he went on to insist that the world had always been guided by inspired persons; variously conceived of according to the intelligence of their times, but whether deities, prophets, or simple men of letters, always heroes. "The history of what man has accomplished in this world is at bottom the history of the great men who have worked here." This directly challenged the prevalent theories of the day, the equality not only of rights but of capacities, the levelling property ascribed to education. In Carlyle's view every great man was great by the grace of God; no human recipe could fashion such an one. "He is as lightning out of Heaven: the rest of men wait for him like fuel, and then they too will flame." The lectures had been most successful when delivered. "Men," said Maurice, "were ranting and canting after Carlyle in all directions." He himself had judged them his "bad best," but the repulsive labour of putting them on paper disgusted him with them. "Nothing I have ever

written pleases me so ill. They have nothing new,
nothing that to me is not old. The style of them requires to be low-pitched, as like talk as possible." He
liked them much better in proof, and declared that they
would astonish the people. They appeared early in
1841 : six lectures treating respectively of the hero as
divinity (Odin) ; as prophet (Mahomet) ; as poet (Dante,
Shakespeare) ; as priest (Luther, Knox) ; as man of
letters (Johnson, Rousseau, Burns) ; as king (Cromwell,
Napoleon).

However the matter may have stood in 1841, in 1887
"Hero Worship" is likely to be read with great admiration but little astonishment. The stars in their courses
have fought for Carlyle. The influence of great or
reputed great men upon politics and thought has been
so enormous, the impotence of the most respectable
causes without powerful representatives has been so no-
torious, that the personal element in history has regained
all the importance of which it had been deprived by the
study of general laws. The problem of harmonizing it
with the truth of general laws remains without solution
from Carlyle. He simply ignores these laws, and as-
sumes that the hero appears when God pleases, and acts
as pleases himsel.. It is also difficult to square the
truth of "Hero Worship" with the truth of "Sartor
Resartus." Carlyle insists with as much energy as ever
that "this so solid-looking material world is, at bottom,
in very deed, Nothing ; is a visual and tactual manifestation of God's power and presence—a shadow hung out by
Him on the bosom of the void Infinite ; nothing more."
This seems to merge all human agency in Divine agency,

and to reduce all heroic action to illusion. The contradiction can undoubtedly be reconciled, but not Carlyle nor another has yet shown how. There is moreover a certain unveracity inherent in Carlyle's method, which the most candid man in his place could not have escaped. He could not avoid treating his heroes individually : and hero worship, directed to an individual, is necessarily an intolerant creed. The votary can have no mercy on the hero's enemies. If he remarks that they too had their place and fulfilled their function in the great scheme, he becomes a Laodicean or Sadducee. Luther's champion can but trample on "the Pagan Pope," Leo ; yet he thus tramples on the flower of a long evolution, always tending towards the light. John Sterling afterwards wrote frcm Rome, which Carlyle never saw : "The depth, sincerity, and splendour that there once was in the semi-paganism of the old Catholics comes out in St. Peter's." Sincerity ! according to Carlyle the chief note of the hero ! All that can be said is that as the injustice lay not in Carlyle's will but in the nature of his task, and as we cannot forego his righteous panegyric of Luther, Pope Leo must find an apostle of equal power —if he can. Carlyle's book—echoed by all the best minds of his day—has been of inestimable service in raising the general level of feeling ; in destroying the shallow sneer, corrosive of all nobleness, that " no one is a hero to his valet-de-chambre ; " in enforcing the truth that " Never from lips of cunning fell the thrilling Delphic oracle." For Cromwell he had yet to fight a hard battle ; but no one, since he wrote, has cast a stone at Mahomet. Niches in his Pantheon are vacant ; he has no place for the Hero as Man of Science or Artist. It is related that, fascinated by the grand figure of Michael Angelo, he once announced his intention of writing his life. It was suggested that some preliminary knowledge of Art might be requisite. "Pooh!" said Carlyle, "what can that signify?" Discerning on reflection that Michael Angelo's architecture and sculpture could not well be omitted from his biography, he gave up the idea, thus confessing, as well as by the gap in "Hero Worship," that he did not see his way to identify plastic Art with the moralities which alone interested him—

> " The unfinished window in Aladdin's tower
> Unfinished must remain."

"Hero Worship" had been too much for Carlyle: he shirked working on his "Cromwell," and went to Yorkshire on a visit to Milnes. He always "wanted to fly into some obscurest cranny" after finishing a book; and, if we can believe him, was regardless of admonitions from very exalted quarters. "The devil reproaches me dreadfully, but I answer, 'True, boy; no sorrier scoundrel in the world than lazy I. But what help? I love no subject so as to give my life for it at present. I will not write on a subject, seest thou? but prefer to ripen or rot for a while.'" Very much more small beer has been chronicled respecting his domestic habits than will be retailed by us. The most interesting circumstance is his nervous horror of noise, which took substance in a sound-proof study. He made dyspepsia bearable by constant exercise on foot and horseback. Light mental occupation was furnished by his preface to Emerson's essays published this year. " This is a world worth abiding in," wrote George Eliot on reading it, "while one man can thus venerate and love another." Emerson's spiritual Muse indeed appears to advantage—

> " Leaning on her grand heroic brother
> As in a picture in some old romaunt."

Carlyle had said to Emerson, "A pen expresses about as much of a man's meaning as the stamping of a hoof will express of a horse's meaning." Emerson, sensitively modest, feared he had expressed too much. "A preface from you is a sort of banner or oriflamme, a little too splendid for my occasion. I fancy my readers to be a very quiet, plain, even obscure class — men and women of some religious culture and aspirations—young, or else mystical, and by no means including the great literary and fashionable army who now read your books." Carlyle assured him that his public was truly aristocratic, being of the bravest inquiring minds England had. He gently censured Emerson's principal defect, the inconsecutiveness of his paragraphs—*arena sine calce*, or bags of duck shot instead of beaten ingots, as Carlyle varied the metaphor. With reviving energies, he planned resuming his old connection with the *Edinburgh Review*, by an essay on contemporary French writers, especially George Sand ; but the scheme, from no editorial indisposition this time, ended in nothing. To have seriously attempted it must have taught him something. From casual allusions in his correspondence, it would seem that he made no nicer distinction between Balzac and Sue than William Taylor had made between Goethe and Kotzebue ; and his aversion for George Sand would appear to prove that he knew nothing of the French fashion of marriage-making. If, like the herd of French novelists, she had really been pandering to a perverted taste by stories of adultery, she would none the less have been striving to dry up the fountain of her own immorality by her assaults on the system which produced such a literature. In the main, 1841 was a barren year. The life of Cromwell gave little sign of emerging from the "mess of great dingy folios" in which Mrs. Carlyle described her husband as habitually buried when at home. Two things, however, gave Carlyle pleasure—the success of the London Library, which had been founded by his initiative the year before; and the invitation from a body of Edinburgh students to stand for a Professorship. Carlyle was deeply touched by this proof of his influence with the young, but he had won the ear of the public, and no longer needed a University platform or imprimatur. He could only bid his young admirers to "be scholars and fellow-labourers of mine in things true and manly; so that we may still work in real concert at a distance and scattered asunder, since together it is not possible for us."

The next year opened mournfully. At the end of February news came that Mrs. Carlyle's mother had been striken by apoplexy at her house in Dumfries-shire. Mrs. Carlyle hurried off instantly, but was met on the way by tidings that her mother was no more. She was carried to bed unconscious, and forbidden to proceed further on her journey. Carlyle was obliged to go to Templand himself, and attend to all arrangements connected with the relinquishment of the farm. In his

letters to his wife during his long detention all the
concealed but fathomless springs of his tenderness are
broken up.   His solemn religiousness and awe-struck
resignation reveal what he meant by "worshipping in
the Cathedral of Immensity."

"Whose great laboratory is that?  The hills stand snow-powdered,
pale-bright.  The black hailstorm awakens in them, rushes down
like a black swift ocean-tide, valley answering valley; and again the
sun blinks out; and the poor sower is casting his grain into the
furrow, hopeful he that the Zodiac and far Heavenly Horologes
have not faltered; and that there will be yet another summer added
for us and another harvest.  Our whole heart asks with Napoleon :
'Messieurs, who made all that?'  Be silent, foolish *Messieurs!*"

Under the influence of such thoughts, his meditation
takes a tinge of mournful, mystic tenderness.   "The old
hills and rivers, the old earth in her star firmaments and
burial vaults, carry on a mysterious unfathomable dialogue
with me."  All things appear in a softer light.  Mrs. Welsh
had not always harmonized with her daughter, much less
with her son-in-law; but, says Carlyle : "How all the
faults and little infirmities of the departed seem now what
they really were, mere virtues imprisoned, obstructed in the
strange, sensitive, tremulous element they were sent to
live in!"   Observing some stone-mason's errors in the
epitaph of his wife's grandfather, he borrowed a hammer
and chisel, and corrected them himself.  By her mother's
death Mrs. Carlyle regained possession of the property,
about £200 a year, which she had renounced in her
parent's favour.   "Oh, Jeanie," exclaims Carlyle, "what
a blessing for us now that we fronted poverty instead of

her doing it! Could the Queen's Treasury compensate us, had we basely left her to such a struggle?"

On his way home Carlyle visited Dr. Arnold, one of the warmest admirers of "The French Revolution," and was conducted by him over the battlefield of Naseby; of which, however, he got no right notion till it was explained to him by his friend Edward Fitzgerald, the translator of Omar Khayyam, and son of the then owner. Later in the year he made a short trip to Belgium with the Bullers, and soon afterwards laid "Cromwell" aside for the time to write "Past and Present." Before treating of this, it may be well to finish the tale of his peregrinations by the mention of an interesting visit to Wales in the summer of the following year. Mr. Charles Redwood, of Llandough, near Cardiff, had been deeply stirred by "Chartism," and had followed out the train of thought thus suggested in an essay, which he had sent to the *Examiner.* Fonblanque making no speed to insert it, Redwood invoked the mediation of Carlyle, and got the precept: "Do not regret if they refuse you — perhaps rejoice rather." The correspondence was continued, and Carlyle made a discovery: "You are not the first estimable and honest man who, with a sardonic triumph, has announced himself to me as an attorney." Redwood pressed Carlyle to visit him, and the invitation coinciding with another from Bishop Thirlwall, the visit was paid in 1843, and liked sufficiently to be repeated. Carlyle found much to admire in his host's sterling character, as well as in the Glamorganshire "green network of intricate lanes, mouldering ruins, vigorous vegetation good and bad," a sketch expanded into a magnificent landscape in his "Life of Sterling." Bending northward on his way back to town, he paid his visit to Thirlwall, who "led me incessantly about in search of the picturesque on high-trotting horses in all weathers; conversation wise, but not restful." Thirlwall had been perplexed about finding people to meet him. They would all identify him with Richard Carlile, so frequently prosecuted for profane libels, "and I thought," added the bishop mischievously, "that Carlyle's conversation would tend to confirm the impression."

Emerson had remarked to Carlyle that "Chartism" was but a breaking of new ground. "It stands as a pre-liminary word, and you will one day, when the fact is riper, read the Second Lesson." The Chartist riots of 1842 did much to ripen both facts and Carlyle's reflections. By October his mind was seething with thought on the condition of "the English nation all sitting enchanted, the poor enchanted so that they can-not work, the rich enchanted so that they cannot enjoy." (Emerson.) "Past and Present" was written during the first seven weeks of 1843, and published in April. The "Past" of the book is the England of Joceline de Brakelonde, chronicler of the Abbey of St. Edmund's Bury at the close of the twelfth century, whose record, published by the Camden Society, had fascinated Carlyle. He may have designed a contrast between the more regulated life of mediæval England and the individualism of his own day, but if so, he must have found that the middle age would need much idealizing. Such a fanciful preference would have suited the retrospicient Newman, whose unspoken prayer had ever been, "Imagination, be thou my Reason." Newman had celebrated in language of incomparable beauty "the great calm, the beautiful pageant, the brotherhood of holy pastors, the stately march of blessed services, heaven let down on earth, the fiends of darkness chased away to their prison below." Alas! if fiends were scarce, fiendish oppressors were plentiful. Carlyle saw that England's needs were secular: and Newman's ideals intrinsically poor. "Anselm by no means included in him all forms of Divine blessing: there were far other forms withal, which he little dreamed of, and William Redbeard was unconsciously the representative and spokesman of these. In truth, could your divine Anselm, your divine Pope Gregory, have had their way, our Western World had all become a European Thibet." Not St. Edmund's Bury Abbey rebuilt, but St. Edmund's Abbot in Downing Street! Carlyle was amply recompensed for his truthfulness. Newman, like Irving before him, grew the more unbelievable the more he believed; until, like many another champion of a lost cause, he fell assassinated by a follower, who, writing under his auspices, added to the memoir of St. Apocryphus, "And this is all that is known, *and more.*" The "Lives of the English Saints" ceased, and have not been republished: but Carlyle's Abbot Samson, "the man of eminent nose, bushy brows, and clear-flashing eyes," is the most authentic piece of the twelfth century extant in the literature of the nineteenth. Yet, though Carlyle displays no sentimental attachment to the middle ages, he makes them too much a foil to the faults of his own. His own account of Samson's election as Abbot proves that the choice might as easily have fallen upon

some tonsured "Pandarus Dogdraught." In truth, Joceline, though a most veracious chronicler, wrote for a
monastic public, and confesses to "tacenda." There is
a more comprehensive picture of somewhat later date
which might have put Carlyle in charity with his contemporaries. If he ever read "The Paston Letters," he there
made the acquaintance of an England infinitely inferior in
public and private virtue to the England of his own day.

The absence of clear connection between Carlyle's
"Past" and his "Present" injures the artistic effect
of his book. There are too many nicknames and
mechanical devices for effect. The metaphor of Plugson's
hundred thousand scalps is excellent, *once.* When the
repetitions are as many as the scalps, it becomes tedious.
Yet the "confused gloom" stigmatized by Mr. Leslie
Stephen is contrasted with fiery splendour. The famous
passage beginning "All true work is sacred," is one of the
noblest Carlyle ever wrote, and not more noble in sentiment
than in rhythm. Nor was his own work empty of result.
Opinion has in the main followed the track pointed out
by Carlyle's luminous finger. Things in being or to be,
from Imperial federation to public washhouses, were
framed or furthered here. The appeal to the aristocracies
of birth and wealth to emulate the aristocracy of worth
has not been entirely unheard. The call for organized
industry under Captain Spade was almost simultaneously
uttered in another dialect by Auguste Comte. Carlyle's
prophecy of the effects of Corn Law and repeal has been
fulfilled to the letter.

"We shall have another period of commercial enterprise, of
victory and prosperity, during which, it is likely, much money will

again be made, and all the people may, by the extant methods, be kept alive and physically fed. The strangling bond of Famine will be loosed from our necks : we shall have room again to breathe, time to bethink ourselves, to repent and consider. A precious and thrice-precious space of years ; wherein to struggle for life in reforming our foul ways ! For our new period or paroxysm of commercial prosperity will, and can, on the old methods of Competition and Devil take the hindmost, prove but a paroxysm."

His principal specific is the organization of labour under "captains of industry " : a suggestive hint towards reconciling the truth of individualism with the truth of socialism. How the enormous interests created by private enterprise are to be dealt with is not clearly indicated. Limited liability was hardly talked of in 1843 ; and Carlyle, intent on his vision of government by the Best, scarcely bestows a thought on the less dazzling but more feasible method of democratic co-operation. Systematized emigration is again a leading point with him, and brings with it the idea of Imperial Federation, "a future wide as the world." " England's sure markets will be among new colonies of Englishmen in all quarters of the globe." The pith of the book is summed up in the beatitude, " Blessed is he who has found his work; let him ask no other blessedness."

Some of Carlyle's followers, recognizing the worth of his thinking, have blamed Government for giving him no opportunity for doing. It has been deemed that he might have worked wonders at a Board of Education. It would have been wonderful if he could have worked at all with two other people in the room. The Government official need not necessarily be "barren, red-tapish, limited, and even intrinsically dark and small," but he must know the meaning of conciliation, compromise, concession. Mill has described the beneficial influence of official employment in his own case, but Carlyle was not Mill. Could he like the East India Company's official have consented to "become one wheel among many"? Could he have learned "instead of being indignant or dispirited when I could not have entirely my own way, to be pleased and encouraged when I could have the smallest part of it"? Official life was not for him : but his influence with official persons was extended by the enlargement of his circle of acquaintances. "I remember," says one who knew him intimately, "no such conflux of notables and nobodies round any other man." It was rather his misfortune than his fault that so few of his acquaintanceships matured into friendships. With one living so exclusively in the intellectual life friendship could only be based on a community of conviction. He did not care for weak thinkers, and strong thinkers had convictions of their own. It was wholly his misfortune that his intimacy with Sterling was so much interrupted by the latter's fragile health. He certainly overrated the docility of his disciple, who, unknown to him, burned and re-wrote all the passages of his "Cœur de Lion" ratified by Carlyle's imprimatur. In the main, however, they harmonized, to the sorrow of Sterling's old friends, who could not see that his entrance into the Church had been an impulsive whim, and his exit a mature decision. He had, as he said, taken orders as a nun takes the veil, to get rid of the wicked world. It is impossible, however, not to sympathize deeply with Sterling's former Pythias, Maurice, lamenting the days when Roebuck had always been able to get at Maurice's opinions by making Sterling talk. Maurice himself was constantly bickering with Carlyle, trying to get rid of the suspicion to which he pleads guilty, that Carlyle took him for a sham. Carlyle did not err so egregiously: though he could not perceive that Maurice's moonshine, like Heaven's, made that beautiful which was not so. Maurice on his part thought Carlyle indispensable to the clergy, as the devil to the saints. " He would show them their ignorance and sin." The roll of the Sterling Club includes several of Carlyle's lifelong friends: Milnes, Thirlwall, Venables, Spedding, Tennyson. Tennyson had a grave blemish in Carlyle's eyes: "he wrote verse because the schoolmaster had taught him that it was great to do so." Alas for poor Emerson! who innocently adjured Carlyle "to cherish Tennyson with love and praise, and draw from him whole books full of new verses yet." The outer man he paints like a great artist. " One of the finest men in the world. A great shock of rough dusty-dark hair; bright laughing hazel eyes; massive aquiline face, most massive yet most delicate; of sallow-brown complexion, almost Indian looking; clothes cynically free and easy; smokes infinite tobacco." After which, deviating into the style of Mrs. Hominy, he adds, "His Way is through Chaos and the Bottomless and Pathless." A strange road to a peerage! Mrs. Hominy's creator was also among his friends, "the good, the gentle, highly-gifted, ever-friendly, noble Dickens," who good-naturedly overlooked the fling at himself in " Past and Present " as " Schnuspel, the distinguished novelist." Carlyle appears among the select company of listeners to the first reading of " The Chimes," depicted by Maclise. Dickens's factotum Forster was also a trusty friend, and kept him supplied with books on the English Commonwealth, as Mill had with books on the French Revolution. Henry Taylor he found "a man of marked veracity, in every sense of that far-reaching word." M. Rio, the apostle of mediæval sentiment, thought how well his *eau sucreé* mixed with Carlyle's usquebaugh, as he heard Carlyle award Peter the Hermit the palm over Demosthenes. Mazzini was much in Cheyne Row, encouraged by Mrs. Carlyle, but shorn of his just dimensions in her husband's eyes by the latter's obstinate indifference to the world's concerns outside the British isles. Mazzini further fretted him by " incoherent Jacobinism, George Sandisms, and other Rousseau fanaticisms." Not all these isms, however, nor "the solidarity of peoples " itself, nor the rest of "the immense nonsense that lay in this brave man," could blind Carlyle to the beauty of the " swift, yet still, Ligurian figure; merciful and fierce ; true as steel, the word and thought of him limpid as water, by nature a little lyrical poet." This was written while Mazzini was besieged in Rome : when after twenty-one years the Italian banner for the second time waved from St. Angelo, Carlyle could but add, " After all, he succeeded." Young men were now beginning to resort to him, as of old to Coleridge. Among them, the most perfect type of loyal allegiance halting short of absolute discipleship, was David Masson.

As Carlyle gained Masson he lost an older and a closer friend. He had long seen that Sterling's life was but "a burning up of him by his own fire." The hunted existence, shunning Death now in Italy, now in the Isle of Wight, was yet further darkened by calamity. Wife and mother died within two days of each other, April, 1843. Some hints in Caroline Fox's diary seem to suggest that consolation might have been had, if Sterling could have lived for it. But near the beginning of September, 1844, came to Carlyle letters, "brief, stern, and loving, altogether noble, never to be forgotten in this world." In return, "there was a note from Carlyle," wrote Sterling to Hare, "I think the noblest and tenderest thing that ever came from human pen." A few days later Carlyle received "verses, written for myself alone, as in star-fire and immortal tears." On September 18th, Sterling passed out of life, to be enrolled with Edward King and Arthur Hallam in the select list of those who have owed their fame to their friends.

## CHAPTER VII

"NOBODY can find work easily if much work do lie in him." This aphorism of Carlyle's, contestable in its general application, was true as concerned himself. Except when in the Berserker passion which had wrung "Past and Present" out of him in seven weeks, he experienced the greatest difficulty in getting hold of a subject. "New things, and as yet no dialect for them." He might almost be compared to Coleridge, of whom it was said that no sooner did anything present itself to him in the form of a duty than he felt incapable of fulfilling it. Carlyle felt the incapacity, and yet fulfilled the duty; with an ungraciousness, however, that, in spite of hearty admiration for his valiant tenacity, will sometimes remind us of Emerson's "Crump, with his grudging resistance to all his native fiends." The composition of his "Cromwell" was long an almost hopeless battle with the fiend Dryasdust. "Four years of abstruse toil, obscure speculations, futile wrestling, and misery." His failure brought out defects in his intellectual equipment. His interest in history was too exclusively human interest. The English Revolution was grievously deficient in the vivid memoirs which had made the French Revolution so attractive a study. Its literature, nevertheless, abounded in pamphlet material which would have enchanted one able to find a picturesque side to everything, or one whose brain was thoroughly magnetized by a great subject. Carlyle could see no picturesqueness and feel no magnetism apart from personal character. Without the least affectation, but to the amazement of other students of the Civil War Tracts, he moans over " huge piles of mouldering wreck," " unspeakable puddlings and welterings," " a sorcerer's dance of extinct human beings and things." A more serious disability still was his disesteem for the hero as constitutional lawyer. Vane, some think, was no less than Cromwell the saviour of the Commonwealth; but, as fast as Cromwell kindled Carlyle, Vane and his like put him out. He knew that he was striving to write an epic rather than a history, and for once wished that he could write in rhyme. He procured a shin bone and sundry teeth from Naseby battlefield, but even these relics proved devoid of virtue. Perhaps they were Royalist. After long struggles, provisionally renouncing the attempt to construct a history from the documents before him, he restricted himself to the arrangement of Cromwell's own letters and speeches, filling up the gaps with a connecting narrative and comment. This was intended merely as a preliminary scaffolding : but when it was done he found that all was done. The egg stood on end. Columbus saw land. The " Letters and Speeches of Oliver Cromwell" was finished on August 26, 1845, and published in December. A second edition was required by May, 1846.

The present biographer can but commend the method

of Carlyle's "Cromwell," for it is his own. He has
deemed it conducive to his reader's pleasure and the
accuracy of his hero's portrait to employ as much as
possible Carlyle's own incomparably vivid language,
using his own mainly to obviate solution of continuity.
Whereas, however, Carlyle's silk is thus darned with
worsted, Cromwell's worsted is darned with silk. There
is a great difference between Cromwell the writer and
Cromwell the speaker. As a writer he is generally
clear, not seldom terse and pungent. As a speaker he
is tortuous and indistinct, obscure sometimes with a
laboured reticence, as though he sought to avoid
speaking out his full mind. " Not defective," says Hume,
" in any talent except elocution." Invaluable as a complete edition of his letters and speeches must have been
to the historical student, it would never have reached the
general reader but for Carlyle's commentary. No method
of exhibiting Cromwell as he was could have been so
effective : the student only needs to remember that it is
necessarily incomplete. The biographer who confines
himself solely to his hero's published utterances makes
his hero his master. " Whither thou goest I will go."
For instance, the execution of Charles I. is almost the
central fact in Cromwell's life, and our opinion of its
justice or policy must colour our entire view of him.
Cromwell, however, has not spoken or written of it :
Carlyle, therefore has nothing to offer, except an obvious
commonplace. His opinion is easily collected from the
drift of his commentary : but there is nothing like a
general weighing of the question, nothing that anticipates
the function of a luminous narrator and dispassionate

judge like Mr. Gardiner. Carlyle's work has been to enable the reader to bring notions about Cromwell to the simplest and sharpest test. Hume believes in Cromwell's sincerity: he was the honest representative of an age of incredible foolishness. " He was at bottom as frantic an enthusiast as the worst of them, and in order to obtain their confidence, needed but to display those vulgar and ridiculous habits which he had early acquired, and on which he set so high a value." Clarendon says briefly, ".He will be looked upon by posterity as a brave wicked man." Southey, with singular want of imagination, enthrones his own conscience in Cromwell's bosom, and makes him die of remorse for his regicide. To Forster he is a noble patriot in the first half of his career, and a liberticidal usurper in the second. Carlyle brings these various conceptions to the test of Cromwell's own words, as to the spear of Ithuriel. The vindication is least complete a asgainst Forster, for in this part of Oliver's life we lose his downright pithy letters, and come to the speeches which even with Carlyle's commentary, appear to most modern readers rambling and confused. When, however, it is remembered that Cromwell's conduct had the approval of so stern a republican as Milton, it will probably be deemed that it must have been enjoined by the necessities of the times. (" Here is a Conscript Father voting in a very pregnant manner.") The letters go as far as could possibly be expected from occasional correspondence to vindicate the writer from other charges. Magnanimity and mercy shine forth with a brightness fully effacing the worst imputations against him. It is impossible that such a man could have exer-

cised such rigour in Ireland without a well-founded conviction that timely severity would prove leniency in the
long run.   Carlyle's pains are to this extent productive,
and his effort triumphant.   Whether Oliver was the perfect saint and perfect ruler that he paints him is another
question.   Such a combination is rare.   It existed in
Marcus Aurelius, but among the royal saints of later
days Louis IX. is perhaps the only one who has not
owed his canonization to his imbecility.   We may
perhaps be content with the judgment of the wise
and impartial Thirlwall : " I firmly believe that Cromwell's convictions were deep, and general aims high
and pure.   But of him it may be said that the intensity
of his earnestness was the very cause of his insincerity.
He lived habitually in a state of exaltation, which could
not be constantly maintained, and I am afraid that he
is often fell into conventionality and insincerity."   What
seemed absurd to Hume seemed august to Thirlwall.
Nothing is more significant of the difference between
the eighteenth and the nineteenth centuries than their
respective constructions of the word *enthusiasm.*

Carlyle's constant walking in his hero's shadow impairs
the merely literary merit of his work.   He had few such
opportunities as in his "French Revolution."   What
pictures he would have given of Charles I. on the
scaffold, or Charles II. in the oak !   The fire, nevertheless, is there, flashing through every aperture it can find.
A superb night-piece, for instance, this of the vigil of
Dunbar.

"And so the soldiers stand to their arms, or lie within instant
reach of their arms, all night.   The night is wild and wet—2nd of

September means 12th by our calendar—the Harvest Moon wades deep among the clouds of sleet and hail. We English have some tents, the Scots have none. The hoarse sea moans bodeful, swinging low and heavy against these whinstone bays; the sea and the tempests are abroad, all else asleep but we—and there is One who rides on the wings of the wind."

If such pieces of description are rare, the comment abounds with sallies in Carlyle's most characteristic style. The Rev. Mark Noble, labouring under carnal inability to apprehend spiritual metaphors, interprets some expressions in an early letter of Cromwell's into a confession of dissoluteness.

"O my reverend imbecile friend," fiercely demands Carlyle, "hadst thou thyself never any moral life, but only a sensitive and digestive? Thy soul never longed towards the serene heights all hidden from thee; and thirsted as the hart in dry places where no waters be? It was never a sorrow for thee that the eternal pole-star had gone out, or veiled itself in thick clouds; a sorrow only that this or the other noble Patron forgot thee when a living fell vacant?"

Poor, well-meaning Noble; to have become a vessel of wrath!

The Cromwell epic had a comic afterpiece in the "Squire Letters." William Squire, a Norfolk man, who introduced himself to Carlyle in January, 1847, deluded him into publishing in *Fraser*, and afterwards in his third edition, a number of letters purporting to be written by Cromwell, the originals of which Squire affirmed that he had himself destroyed in a sulky fit. Carlyle should have seen the improbability of this tale, and his deportment

towards the critics who didsee it can only be described
as peevish and ostrich-like. He would have less easily
become Squire's dupe if hehad known nothing of him
personally, but he had mad an attentive and as far as it
went an accurate study of ne man, and was misled by
compassion for a fellow-creaure so evidently on the road
to Bedlam. But Squire wa crafty as well as crazy, and
had dabbled both in archœology and fabrication more
than Carlyle wotted of. The letters, after all, were insignificant, in itself a suspicious circumstance. The little
internal evidence they yieded was damnatory. Cromwell, *apud* Squire, "regres much that worthy vessel of
the Lord, Sprigg, came to hurt." Where was Carlyle's
sense of the absurd?

Carlyle's work on the Civil War Pamphlets, though
mainly performed by the aid of "a hardy intelligent
amanuensis," had brought him into contact with the
British Museum authorites, and led to his being ex-
amined before the Museum Commissioners in 1849.
His evidence, at present buried in a Blue Book, should
be read, for it is probably the most sustained specimen
of his talk extant. It is also most illustrative both of his
strength and his weakness. Excellent is his application
of hero worship to practical affairs.

"You must have a man to direct who knows well what the duty
is that he has to do ; and who is determined to go through that, in
spite of all the clamour raised against him ; and who is not anxious to
obtain approbation, but is satisfied that he will obtain it by-and-by,
provided that he acts ingenuously and faithfully."

He could have drawn no better portrait of Panizzi, the

actual librarian, a hero of administration who should have
been a hero after his own heart, but in whom he could
only see a type of the "prurient darkness and confused
pedantry and ostentatious inanity of the world which
put him there." He did not know that Panizzi had
fought against that mismanagement in the case of the
French Revolutionary pamphlets, which had made the
Museum library nearly useless when he himself wrote his
history.[1] This personal matter apart, and allowing for
the physical sensitiveness of this nervous mortal, his
evidence is admirable, including excellent suggestions
since carried into effect, cordial acknowledgments of
services rendered, and humorous sallies against the
nuisances of the Reading-room : "Museum headaches,"
and persons "who blow their noses in an insane manner."
Let the reader of to-day who finds no seat find patience
as he figures to himself Carlyle "obliged to sit on the top
of a ladder." On the question of the selection of books
he naturally leans to the expurgatorial view, drawing,
however, the distinction : "Where I found any kind of
human intellect exercised, even though the man was a
blockhead, I would not reject his book. But when the
man was a *quack*, I should consider that I was doing
God service in extinguishing such a book."

In the autumn of 1847 Emerson came to lecture in
England, guided by "the broad sagacity and practicality"
of Alexander Ireland, who, "infinitely well affected towards the man Emerson," had undertaken the burden of
all business arrangements. The friendship sworn be-

[1] "Croker Papers," vol. ii. p. 283.

tween Emerson and Carlyle on the strength of a few
hours' intercourse, had since been cemented by the
former with the most disinterested and delicate kindnesses.　The course of years, however, had not brought
them to the same path in their intellectual wayfarings.
Carlyle had become more than ever a prophet, Emerson
more than ever a sage.　Carlyle had always been dis-
dainfully intolerant of the genus of Socrates, Marcus
Aurelius, and Channing.　It is not surprising that he
beheld in its representative under his own roof "a gym-
nosophist sitting idle on a flowery bank "—a comparison
he had previously used of Novalis.　Caroline Fox says
that he tried to shake Emerson's optimism by taking
him the round of all the horrors and abominations of
London, asking after each exhibition, "Do you believe in
the devil now?"　But Emerson "had every day a better
opinion of the English."　He was never disposed to
conclude "that is impossible, because it is too beautiful,"
preferring to think that, "on the contrary, it was too
beautiful not to be possible."[1]　Carlyle, on his side,
grimly admitted that there was good in everything: if
you even saw Oliver Cromwell assassinated, it was certain
you could get a load of turnips from his carcase.　This
consoling truth must nevertheless have been forgotten,
else Emerson had not been sent to preach it so em-
phatically !　He observed that the optimistic Milnes

---

[1] Mary Hennell's quotation from an unnamed "disciple of
Fourier" in her appendix to Charles Bray's "Philosophy of
Necessity."　George Eliot, writing some time afterwards to Mary
Hennell's sister, says: "There is a sort of blasphemy in that
proverbial phrase, 'Too good to be true.'"

was only fit to be "Perpetual President of the Heaven
and Hell Amalgamation Society." But he meant only
half he said. He enjoyed denouncing the Americans as
eighteen millions of bores, but he was seriously distressed
when the eighteen-millionth fraction of the nation refused
to call upon him. Better the united boredom of the
United States than one such just rebuke. Nothing is
more conclusive of his affectionate nature than his agitation when he fears that his spleen may have alienated
his friend. He deprecates, adjures, almost coaxes.
"Has not the man Emerson, from old years, been a
Human Friend to me? Can I ever think otherwise than
lovingly of the man Emerson?" "You are a blessing
to me on this earth; no letter comes from you with other
than good tidings—or can come while you live there to
love me." Emerson was not the man to be obdurate.
He proved that his optimism was no fruit of imbecility
by the soundness and insight of his judgment of
Carlyle. He saw that Carlyle's literary genius was but
a minor accompaniment of his moral nature, "an
Æolian attachment to an enormous trip-hammer."
"There is more character than intellect in every sentence." He was struck by Carlyle's affinity to Johnson,
but observed that the step which England had made
from one to the other was prodigious. "If she can
make another step as large, what new ages open!"

Emerson's lectures were a great success, and he mixed
with the best English intellectual society, hearing, among
other things, a demolition of the "Squire Letters" from
Macaulay. Carlyle replied as he read his rival's History,
"Flow on, thou shining river!" The hit was fair and

penetrant : but he ought not to have overlooked Macaulay's almost unique power of kindling patriotic emotion,
and making his reader a better citizen. He was prejudiced alike against the historian and the " scandalous
period " of his narrative, forgetting that " in our Father's
house are many mansions." He made several interesting
visits about this time, especially to Lord and Lady
Ashburton, whose intimacy was to bring momentous
consequences. He went to Malvern, where Dr. Gully's
warm welcome did him more good than his cold water ;
and to Lancashire, where he fore-gathered with John
Bright. The philosopher and the orator should have
confined their discourse to George Fox, Milton, and
Cromwell. For want of this precaution harmony was
not attained : months afterwards Carlyle's thunder still
rumbled in the ears of the good people of Rochdale.
Bright's stature had not yet risen, as it was to rise, to
Carlyle's standard of the heroic. Carlyle accepted
Free Trade, but not as a gospel. " I will not fire
guns when this small victory is gained. I will re-
commend a day of fasting rather, that such a victory
required such gaining." He continued his visits to his
brother James, "the express image of my father in his
ways of living and thinking;" and wrote of his decrepid
mother : " It is beautiful to see affection surviving
where all else is submitting to decay; the altar with its
sacred fire still burning while the outer walls are all
slowly crumbling." The stroke so long suspended here
fell with crashing suddenness on another head. Charles
Buller died on November 29, 1848. "There," cried
Thackeray, "go wit, fame, friendship." With Buller

also went Carlyle's chief hold upon public men. "In the coming storms of trouble," he wrote in the beautiful tribute which he paid his friend in the *Examiner*, "one radiant element will be wanting now."

Carlyle had written powerfully in "Chartism" of the leprosy of Irish wretchedness for which England was so largely responsible, and which "by the aid of steam and modern progress of the sciences, has now crept over to us and become our own wretchedness." He had noticed Pat "in Piccadilly, blue-visaged, thatched in rags, a blue child on each arm; hunger-driven, wide-mouthed, seeking whom he may devour." He had written of Repeal in the *Examiner* and *Spectator*, treating it as self-evident that "England's job of work, inexorably needful to be done, cannot go on at all unless her back-parlour belong to herself."

"If in the present cowardly humour of most ministers and governing persons and loud insane babble of anarchic men, a traitorous minister did consent to help himself over the evil hour by yielding, even he, whether he saved his traitorous head or lost it, could have done nothing towards the Repeal of the Union. An Eternal Law proclaims the Union irrepealable in these centuries."

He now determined to see Ireland for himself. The record of the tour he made in the summer of 1849, never intended for publication, given away, passed from hand to hand, was eventually published in 1882. Divers tart remarks on harmless people should have been omitted, but we could ill have spared it. It is the climax of perceptive and descriptive power. Carlyle's reader has seen the Ireland of 1849. Nothing seems to have

struck him so much as the general patchiness of the
country, crag, bog, field, misery, jollity, industry, unthrift,
lying side by side, sharply defined as the squares in a
chess-board. "The whole country figures in my mind
like a ragged coat, not patchable any longer." "Which
quack of us is not to blame for it?" If he had any
preconceived views on Irish difficulties, they broke down
in the presence of facts. At the end of his tour he
could propound no other recipe for Irish regeneration
than that "Irishmen should cease generally from following the devil." This honest utterance may not have
endeared him to Irish readers: yet it would argue a
dulness infrequent in the Emerald Isle to overlook his
affection and compassion; his hearty sympathy for every
fellow man in whom he finds a ray of light, and his
absolute struggle to put the most favourable construction
on all such; his joy when, "the imagination drowned in
black desolation for fifteen miles past," he comes to as
much as "an incipient farm." It must be remembered
that he wrote before the Encumbered Estates Act had
brought some capital into the country, and that, though
making nearly a complete circuit of the island, he did
not visit the best grazing districts. Changes have come
since, for better and worse. If the writer may trust his
own observation, mendicancy is much less general than
formerly in the eastern part of the country: it is morti-
fying, on the other hand, to be assured that the old love
of literature is withering, seared by vitriolic newspapers.
Carlyle would have grieved sorely over this symptom.
Education was the one point on which he was in accord
with the philanthropists. "If the devil," he says in this

book, "were passing through my country, and he applied to me for instruction on any truth or fact of this universe, I should wish to give it him."

The infirmity of his mother, deaths and estrangements among friends, domestic sorrows as yet untold, discontent with public affairs intensified by the dismal impressions of his Irish tour, had made the world very heavy for Carlyle by the autumn of 1849. "I am very weary," he says, "and the more sleep I get I seem to grow the wearier. All the old tremulous affection lies in me, but it is as if frozen." There is but one way of deliverance from such a condition; man must "cleanse his bosom of the perilous stuff," either by thought or action. Intent in good faith on "mending his shell with pearl," Carlyle turned to the "masses of written stuff which he grudged a little to burn," though feeling them "wrongish, every word of them." The first fruit of his revision was the "Occasional Discourse on the Nigger Question," which appeared in *Fraser* for December, 1849. Twelve more objurgations had been prescribed, but eight were found to suffice. ("O ye Gauchos, South American and European, what a business is it, casting out your seven devils!") These "Latter-Day Pamphlets," discussing "The Present Time, Model Prisons, Downing Street, The New Downing Street, The Stump Orator, Parliaments, Hudson's Statue, and Jesuitism," appeared between January and July, 1850. The coincidence of the discontinuance of the series with the death of Sir Robert Peel, with whom Carlyle had lately cultivated friendly relations, and a subsequent remark of his own, confirm the belief that he had at this time serious thoughts of entering public

life.  Peel could probably have helped him to a seat:
but had he duly pondered late sittings and the importunities of constituents?   In essential points he was
much better qualified for St. Stephen's than for Downing
Street; he might perhaps, as Mill did afterwards, have
materially raised the Commons in the estimation of
thinking men.   To judge by his Museum evidence, he
would have adapted himself to the situation, and spoken
with due observance of ceremony, rivetting his hearers'
attention as his vivid phrases sped arrow-straight to the
mark.   He showed no such adaptability in his "Latter-
Day" discourses, which are mainly cast in an oratorical
mould.   But he wrote in his study, alone with his anger,
his grief, and his biliousness.   It was the hey-day of the
commercial school of politics, with its cash-book and its
calico, its proscription of sentiment, its abandonment of
the colonies, its general tendency to ignore the duties
and abdicate the functions of government.   Reaction
has supervened; Carlyle might say now that legislation
has mainly followed the path he indicated; and that
where it has not precisely done so—as in the case of
reform in Downing Street—his end has been sought by
other means.   Few of the ideas so tempestuously expressed in these pamphlets, nevertheless, are new ideas
with him; the brandy is out of all proportion to the
bread.   Professor Masson ably brought out the strong
points in his article in the *North British Review*
(November, 1850).   He could not say much for the
" Occasional Discourse on the Nigger Question."   Not
to have seen that the harshest iron of slavery entered
not black but white souls: that compulsory labour must

make all labour infamous and all pride in work impossible, was a strange blindness. Carlyle meditated another pamphlet, on Bibliolatry, to be entitled, "Exodus from Houndsditch." "But Pallas came in shape of rust." He should have written it earlier, when poorer in mannerisms and richer in caution and considerateness; but he had not then fully grasped the subject. "Si jeunesse savait et si vieillesse pouvait"—an old tale!

We have deferred till now the mention of one of Carlyle's most brilliant and characteristic performances, as it strikingly exemplifies both the worth and the un-worth of his "Latter-Day" gospel. If the "lean and iron" Dictator of Paraguay, Dr. Francia, was what Carlyle thought him when he wrote upon him in 1843, he was a very remarkable man. If he was "a fool with malignity dominating his character," as Mr. Washburn thought in 1871, he was a much more remarkable man. To us he seems a kind of South American Frederick, except in military talent. Fool or Frederick, he obtained such perfect control of a people already well drilled by the Jesuits, that when an unworthy successor came to authority he found, witness Colonel Thompson, "that the robbery of the treasury was a thing impossible to be done in Paraguay except by himself." An ideal seldom attained by a Frederick, and surely never by a fool. During his government and that of his successor, Carlos Lopez, however private interests might suffer from the rapacity of the chief of the State, the State itself was a pattern of order, realizing Carlyle's ideal of the Sufficient Man with the sufficient stick in the midst of South American anarchy—

"Via prima salutis,
Quod minime reris, Graia pandetur ab urbe."

So perfect was the mechanism that it worked as ad-
mirably as ever when in process of time it came into
the hands of a monster without one particle of sense, or
one vestige of a virtue. Francia and Carlos Lopez had
commanded Paraguay to renounce intercourse with
foreign nations, and Paraguay had obeyed. Solano
Lopez commanded her to challenge neighbouring nations
to a war of extermination, and Paraguay obeyed again.
Every drop of blood, every farthing of money, every
resource of intelligence the land could produce; devotion unutterably pathetic, valour unsurpassed in the
history of any people; were lavished at the insane
bidding of the worst man not only in the country, but
upon the earth. When the end had come:

"Of the four hundred and fifty thousand females in Paraguay at
the commencement of the war not sixty thousand were left alive.
Of the males, including the boys under ten years of age, there were
not twenty thousand. Of full-grown men capable of bearing arms,
there could not have been ten thousand; so that after this terrible
war there was left alive, of the whole Paraguayan nation, but one-
tenth of its population."

This was in 1870. Carlyle had lived long enough to
know that the despotism of the Sufficient may be the
greatest of curses, unless it can be prevented from becoming the despotism of the Insufficient, which, from
the very nature of absolute authority, it never can.

# CHAPTER VIII.

THE acrid mood which had envenomed the Latter-Day Pamphlets was not wholly produced by bodily suffering or discontent with the times. From 1846 to 1857 a shadow crept over Carlyle's life, deepening with every step he made towards the tomb, until, save in the ever black retrospect, it suddenly disappeared. "I am infinitely solitary," is his complaint in a letter to Emerson, written in 1852. "Solitary!" Emerson must have asked to himself, "where is Jane Carlyle?" Alas! "the fount of murmuring sparkling living love" had for a season become "a comfortless and hidden well."

Of the various causes which may have contributed to this unfortunate estrangement, only two, an external and a far more subtle internal one, deserve serious attention. By his fitful moods and habitual repining, and his culpable though wholly unconscious neglect of many of his wife's interests and comforts, Carlyle had certainly done enough to provoke any ordinary woman. But Mrs. Carlyle was no ordinary woman, and these things weighed hardly a feather with her until she found that another was giving him what she had not to give. She made this discovery soon after the Carlyles' first visit to Lord and

Lady Ashburton in December, 1845. No intimacy could have seemed, or really been, more innocent. Lady Ashburton was devotedly attached to her husband, of whom Mrs. Carlyle herself speaks in enthusiastic terms. Carlyle was so far from being ashamed of his wife that, contrary to the practice of many men of letters in similar cases, he insisted on taking her with him whenever he visited the Grange, and gloried in what he thought her superiority to every woman of rank and fashion there—except Lady Ashburton. All the mischief lay in that exception. The truth is that, fortunate as their union proved in many respects, Mrs. Carlyle was not the ideal partner for Carlyle. Whether he ought to have married at all is a serious question, not to be raised here. But if he was to marry, his need was a woman who could unseal the hidden tenderness of his nature. No man had more, few so much: but it needed some exterior agent to draw it forth. Professsor Masson says :

"No one who knew Carlyle but must have noted how instantaneously he was affected or even agitated by any case of difficulty or distress in which he was consulted or that was casually brought to his cognizance, and with what restless curiosity and exactitude he would inquire into all the particulars till he had conceived the case thoroughly, and, as it were, taken the whole pain of it into himself."

What might he not have been had he had a companion who could have exercised that influence upon him day by day which the casual encounter with distress did intermittently and by accident ! Mrs. Carlyle, unhappily, was grievously deficient in tenderness, not of deed, but of thought and speech. She was most charitable, most helpful, self-sacrificing, and even delicate in her kindness; but she almost invariably took a hard view of persons and things. Throughout her correspondence scarcely anything can be found with the least tendency to free Carlyle's affectionate nature from its hard envelopment; everything, on the contrary, tended to narrow his sympathies, edge his sarcasms, intensify his negations, and foster his disdain for whatever would not run in his own groove. What wonder that when he emerged at last into a more gracious atmosphere, his heart should open like the leaves of a reviving plant? "In the sunshine of that pleasant region," says Mr. Venables, "all his nature seemed to expand. He was nowhere else so bright, so communicative, and so cheerful; and his conversation rose even above its ordinary standard." Miss Jewsbury (who never saw Lady Ashburton) attributes this renovation to the great lady's "little ways." "Lady Ashburton," replies Mr. Venables, indignantly, "was the most magnanimous of women, and she had no little ways." "The greatest lady of rank I ever saw," testifies Carlyle, "with the soul of a princess and captainess." Mrs. Carlyle's grievance very evidently was not that Lady Ashburton was unworthy of her husband's regard, but that she was far too worthy. Dimly conscious of something wrong, yet only half-apprehending the situation, Carlyle only wanted an excuse for a burst of affection which must have convinced even her how infinitely at the bottom of his heart he preferred her to any other woman. Mrs. Carlyle's rod was not the rod of Moses. It would be almost comical, were it not so tragical, to see this clever, brilliant woman so absolutely stupid over a problem which a genial nature would have instantly solved, adding scoff to scoff and taunt to taunt when nothing was needed but frankness and demonstrative affection to win her more than she had lost. Carlyle took all patiently: his letters have a vague wistful pathos, infinitely touching. A situation that might have become intolerably strained was suddenly terminated by the death of Lady Ashburton, May, 1857. Mrs. Carlyle recovered her good humour: Carlyle, though deeply grieving for his friend, accepted the change at home with passive thankfulness. The domestic sky went on brightening. Storms came once and again, but they were generally provoked by Carlyle's gusts of temper, and vanished with them. Mrs. Carlyle's continued ill-health was a more serious trouble, but it made Carlyle bridle his impetuous moods, and .hink more heedfully of his wife's comfort in external things than he had ever thought before. Had Death come for Mrs. Carlyle a few hours earlier on that fatal 21st of April, 1866, he would have found her writing to her husband as eagerly, cheerfully, and affectionately as in her best days.

This painful chapter has a more painful appendix. How, it may well be asked, can Carlyle's biographer, having no wish and no right to treat of his most intimate affairs, find it his duty to treat of them nevertheless? Carlyle's trusted friend has made it so. Late in life Carlyle collected his wife's letters, but not for publication as they stood. "He warned me," says the literary executor himself, " that before they were published they would require anxious revision. He left me at last with discretion to destroy the whole of them, should I find the task of discrimination too intricate a problem." To no one of right judgment or proper feeling could the " problem " of printing or omitting many things in Mrs. Carlyle's letters and journals have presented any intricacy whatever. To none should it have been less intricate than to Mr. Froude, who had already done Carlyle a grievous wrong by his unrevised edition of the " Reminiscences," and who knew better than any one that any fault of which Carlyle could justly accuse himself had been atoned for a hundred times over. He also knew as well as Professor Masson could inform him, that "he had no right to make free with those most secret self-communings of Mrs. Carlyle's spirit which she had kept under lock and key from Carlyle himself, and which Carlyle himself had no right to treat as property which he could assign away." With all this knowledge, he not only prints the sacred journal and its companion correspondence, but, in Mr. Venables' words, " carefully directs attention to an episode which occupies fewer than twelve pages out of twelve hundred of Mrs. Carlyle's published letters." It is just to add that Mr. Froude's last two volumes, " Carlyle in London," indicate a disposition to repair the mischief he has done, as far as is possible without acknowledging that he has done any.

Who has not seen beneath a storm-swept heaven some patch of green herbage or yellow harvest shine with harmless fire, as sunbeams stream upon it from a rift in the dark sky ? Such a patch of vivid refreshment at this dreary part of Carlyle's life is his biography of John Sterling, written between January and June, 1851, and

published in October.  A work elegiac indeed, the epitaph
of high frustrated hopes, but at once so heroically exult-
ant and so nobly resigned as to leave that impression of
satisfaction and acquiescence which the biographies of
successful men often fail to produce.  Sterling's fortune
was exceptional.  He had achieved little, and with all his
brightness and alacrity of mind, it may be doubted
whether he had enough originality or enough perseverance to have achieved anything very considerable, unless
it had been in oratory.  Yet, such a genius had he for
friendship, that three of the most intellectual men in
England contended for the writing of his life, each from
his own point of view—

> " Tres mihi convivæ prope dissentire videntur,
> Poscentes vario multum diversa palato. "

Mill gave up the intention which he had continued to
entertain for some time after the appearance of Arch-
deacon Hare's memoir : and this, elegant, interesting,
and affectionate as it is, has been completely obliterated
by Carlyle's.  The literary power of the writers was as
disproportionate as the scale on which they wrought ; but
if Hare had commanded Carlyle's genius and materials,
his work must still have been a failure from his miscon-
ception of his business.  To raise a hue and cry after the
bright fleet Sterling as a runaway curate was really no
better than, as Carlyle admonished another person on
another occasion, to upbraid the sun for not lighting one's
cigar.  Carlyle paints Sterling as he really was, "joyous
youth, everlastingly striving"—with his own instability, in
some degree, as well as with Fate and Fortune.  Yet so

attractive is the picture of incessant exalted effort, however desultory, that the general impression is one of almost complete satisfaction. Sterling appears as the representative of a peculiar type of excellence, singled out from the crowd of successful poets and novelists. As a work of art the biography is perfect, "perspicuously planned," sober or copious in detail as the occasion enjoins, and penned in a chastened style which has forfeited none of its strength in parting with most of its abruptness. It required no little skill to insure Sterling due prominence in a book containing such wonderful pictures as those of his father and of Coleridge. Coleridge is decked in purple for the sacrifice ; involuntary homage is rendered to his greatness by making him the central figure of a landscape like this : "Waving blooming country of the brightest green ; dotted all over with handsome villas, handsome groves ; crossed by roads and human traffic, here inaudible or heard only as a musical hum ; and behind all swam, under olive-tinted haze, the illimitable limitary ocean of London." One very amiable feature in the book is Carlyle's vigilant seizure of every opportunity to introduce a kindly notice of Mill, now irretrievably estranged from him. Mill had forgiven the "Philistine Mill" of "Hero Worship," but intellectual divergencies and some inconsiderate speeches of the Carlyles had stifled intercourse. Carlyle foamed against Mill in his diaries, and signalled reconciliation in his books. Mill held on his course, uncomplaining and inflexible. Such is the difference between the poetical and the logical temperaments, respectively incarnated in the two best men of that day.

The success of " Sterling " was a broad hint to Carlyle that the world preferred his stories to his sermons.  He took it at once, never wanting tact in literary matters. About January, 1852, after casting his eyes about, as he told Mr. Symington, for a man that could rule, he fixed upon Frederick the Great, the last of the long line of Protestant heroes beginning with Maurice of Saxony. The choice was in many respects fortunate, but had two disadvantages.  Frederick, though a worthy compeer of Cæsar, was far below the moral standard of heroism which Carlyle had set up in Cromwell: and, with Carlyle's exacting conscience, the task involved endless " hugging of unclean creatures," *i.e.*, reading dull books.  He had called out loudly enough on previous occasions, but as our little insular fights to Leuthen and Rossbach, so are his wails over Cromwell to his howls over Frederick. The pith of them is packed into his complaint to Emerson : "A task that I cannot do, that generally seems to me not worth doing, and that yet must be done.  No job approaching to it in ugliness was ever cut out for me ; nor had I any motive to go on, except the sad negative one, Shall we be beaten in our old days ? "  He had two assistants, without whom he might have failed.  Joseph Neuberg, a highly accomplished and thoughtful German merchant at Nottingham, introduced to him by Emerson, having acquired a competence by trade, offered himself as volunteer secretary, " by way of having a generous employment in this world."  Neuberg accompanied him in a visit to Germany in 1852, and earned the praise of being equal to six couriers.  After the journey Neuberg's worth was appraised at ten couriers, and he improved even upon this character in a second expedition made in 1858. He continued helpful for the remainder of his life, unearthing facts and dates from all manner of burrows, and translating the history itself into German. "No kinder friend," wrote Carlyle when he had lost him, "had I in this world." The other indispensable assistant was Mr. Henry Larkin, who not only vicariously endured much of the pain of "Frederick," but compiled the indexes and summaries which are such invaluable adjuncts to Carlyle's complete works. "You wanted work," Carlyle grimly observed to him, "and are likely to *get* it." Poor Mr. Larkin, for his sins, had a talent for drawing maps and plans, and was expected to be able to indicate the exact position of any marching body of troops at any hour of the day. He was clever in reading crabbed copy, and it devolved upon him to decipher all such portions of Carlyle's manuscript as Carlyle could not decipher himself. On the whole, his position much resembled that of the *famulus* of the demon doctor in "Tales of the Zenana," save that that gentleman's assistant dined much better than Carlyle's. But Yusoof never got that cordial acknowledgment of service rendered by which Carlyle ultimately salved over all soreness, and assigned his secretary a niche in history by the side of Napoleon's and Voltaire's. The first two volumes of the History appeared in 1858, the sixth and last in 1865. Their success was decisive, although Carlyle's seeming apotheosis of mere strength in his portrait of Frederick's father (but he never could help rejoicing over a man when he found him, even though the man were a brute) brought an amusing castigation upon him in Mr. P. P. Alexander's "Smelfungus on Sauerteig," the best of the many parodies of his style.

Carlyle's method in "Frederick" is the reverse of his method in "Cromwell." In "Cromwell" his voice rises and falls with his hero's; when Cromwell is silent, Carlyle is dumb. In "Frederick" he speaks for his hero on an infinity of matters on which his hero spoke not at all. Cromwell's companions stand apart at an awful distance; but Frederick moves in the midst of a multitudinous pageant. Carlyle has ransacked the earth to fill his train. "Quae regio terrae nostri non plena laboris?" Mohawks and Moguls swell the host; philosophers jostle opera dancers; nay, the procession is headed by a troop of Electoral Spectres, alive for the occasion. It would be a prodigious historical masquerade were the characters in domino. But every figure has his own proper visage, stamped indelibly with the expression it bore as he flitted across this earth. Everything aids the picture; some things encumber the history. We shall not complain of Carlyle for giving so much more than he undertook; yet his lament over his labour need not have been so loud, had he realized how large a part of it was self-imposed. Much, it is probable, was an involuntary "mending of his shell with pearl." He had not loved his hero immoderately from the first, and the love he had it pleased Heaven to decrease on further acquaintance. It must have become increasingly clear to him that, notwithstanding traits of magnanimity and tenderness not too common in finer natures, Frederick was practically guided by no other rule of conduct than that which he had himself styled "a vulpine morality." He does his best for Reynard's ethics by representing them as grounded upon an accurate, quite a religious, perception of God's truth in the shape of Fact. But is not this rather in the line of the "Heaven and Hell Amalgamation Society "? If I recognize that my neighbour's watch cannot be at the same time in his pocket and in mine, does veneration for this Eternal Law constrain me to transfer it to the latter? Can I not exhibit my reverence even better by leaving it where it is? Carlyle, in fact, thought so, and the thought spoiled his pleasure in his book. Yet in a great degree he felt himself on solid ground. Frederick's work needed a Frederick. "There are certain devils," declares Cardinal Borgia, "which absolutely can *not* be cast out by holy water." Frederick's unhallowed methods ejected some of them. Here, as usual, Time has fought for Carlyle. He lived to see how much more vitally important Frederick's work had been than he could possibly have imagined when he sat down to write his life. We owe too much to the stout cable by which the vessel of European order now mainly rides, to feel other than grateful to the hand that threw it out, were it even a corsair's. As fighting and planning hero, Frederick is unsurpassable; it did seem an irony of fate that his life should be written by a great moralist. His energy, vigilance, intrepidity, perseverance, sense of duty to his own subjects and generally unconquerable soul receive full justice from his biographer, who is not unmindful either of the peculiar Nemesis he brought upon himself. "In these seven weeks he has, with *gloire* or otherwise, cut out for himself such a life of labour as no man of his century had." The account of Frederick's

restoration of his ruined kingdom should have borne a
larger proportion to that of his battles, but Carlyle was
fagged when the story reached this point.  As a military
historian he is perfectly at home.  Professional readers
extol the science of his battle-pieces, the non-professional
can at least affirm their clearness.  He had been over
every battlefield, and no topographical detail had escaped
him.  For the rest, the book is no sublime epic like "The
French Revolution"; but a many-morselled mosaic of
portrait and incident, sarcasm and apophthegm; full of
things that before Carlyle would have seemed wildly
misplaced in a history; arresting the mind, open it where
you may; haunting it, close it where you will; too long,
presumably, to be much read by posterity; but the
book for the man of one book, were not that species
extinct.

Except for domestic sorrow, the events of Carlyle's
life during his Thirteen Years' War with Frederick
were not momentous.  Driven by workmen out of his
home in 1852, and wisely committing "the tools to her
that could handle them," he escaped on the tour to
Germany previously mentioned.  Besides accomplishing
his special object of collecting materials for "Frederick,"
he sought the shrines of Goethe, Schiller, and Luther;
saw Tieck, "beautiful old man; so serene, so calm, so
sad;" and, as already hinted, enlightened Prussian
pietists as to the proper use of the sun.  In December,
1853, he was hastily summoned to Scotland, just in
time to see his mother ere she expired.  "It was my
mother, and not my mother.  The last pale rim or
sickle of the moon which had once been full, sinking

in the dark seas." The summons had found him at Lord Ashburton's, where he was a frequent visitor, ridding himself of many prejudices, and amazing the company with many paradoxes. "His opinions," says Sir Henry Taylor, "darted about like the monsters of the solar microscope, perpetually devouring each other."

> "If Jack o' Lantern
> Shows you his way, though you should miss your own,
> You ought not to be too exact with him."

Much of Carlyle's manner and conversation about this time is probably reflected in the Saunders Mackaye of "Alton Locke," "that wonderfully splendid and coherent piece of Scotch bravura," as he himself called it. Kingsley afterwards became shy of him, but to the last, when tired or depressed, turned to "The French Revolution." Ruskin came to gaze on the fire which had kindled his own torch; and even Samuel Wilberforce had light enough vouchsafed him to discern that Carlyle was "a most eminently religious man." Dr. Knighton, who was often in his company at this time, found him eruptive of much volcanic matter, especially of complaints that the national talent was now wholly directed to talking and writing, instead of doing. The Indian Mutiny was put down next year, but Carlyle was not. Yet he could tolerate contradiction. He had once spoken of a contemporary poet as a "phrasemonger." "But what," asked another author, "are the best of us but phrasemongers?" "True," said Carlyle. His simplicity and self-absorption sometimes led him into amusing inadvertencies. Sincerely desiring to compliment Browning on

"The Ring and the Book," he remarked, with all serious-
ness: "It's a wonderful book, one of the most wonderful
poems ever written. I re-read it all through—all made
out of an Old Bailey story that might have been told in
ten lines, and only wants forgetting!" He favoured
Prince Napoleon with this proof of the advantage of discipline: "In a few months the ship has become a perfect
machine, worked with undeviating regularity, and if she
meets a Frenchman of her own size she blows him into
atoms." Let us hope that the Prince was as good-natured
as the poet, whose genius has more affinity to Carlyle's than
that of any other contemporary, and who continued his
genial friend and visitor. Young disciples knocked timidly,
suing for a sight of the philosopher, or at the least of his
boots. Americans came and went, squeezing the fingers
of Mrs. Carlyle, "whose rings were all utilitarian and had
seals." Mr. Moncure Conway's sunny picture of Mrs.
Carlyle's bright banter of her husband, and his acquiescence, is expanded in the memoir of the late much loved
and much missed Anne Gilchrist. Mrs. Gilchrist and
her husband, the biographer of Etty and Blake, dwelt
for some time next door to the Carlyles, and Gilchrist
wrought wonders in ferreting out authorities for the
life of Frederick. The memoir has many letters expressive of Carlyle's gratitude and of Mrs. Carlyle's practical
and at the same time delicate sympathy with the widow
on occasion of Gilchrist's sudden death; it has also
touches significant of Mrs. Carlyle's private opinion of her
husband and her way of managing him. ("Between two
and three o'clock is a very placid hour with the creature.")
In consultations respecting the "Frederick" proofs—

the great bane of Carlyle's existence just then—he generally began by calling her a fool, and ended by following her advice. "He never complains of serious things, but if his finger is cut one must hold it and another get plaister." She read aloud the account of the execution of the assassin Buranelli (a step of great propriety). "Tears rolled down Carlyle's cheeks—he who talks of shooting Irishmen who will not work." Mr. Larkin, continually about the house at this time, celebrates Carlyle's royal graciousness of manner and his half-silences, the soothing twilight of his blazing eloquence. "Both Carlyle and Mrs. Carlyle," he adds, "had singularly expressive voices, and yet singularly different from each other, like the many tones of a powerful organ and the perfect modulations of a mellow flute." The picture of the household would be pleasing, even bright with a faint autumnal brightness, but for Mrs. Carlyle's sufferings from neuralgic pain and the unhappy accompanying incidents, a serious street accident, loss of power in the right arm, a dismal journey to St. Leonard's in an invalid's carriage, which resembled a coffin ordered in anticipation. She had, nevertheless, rallied surprisingly shortly before her death. Carlyle, tardily, but not too tardily thoughtful, made her take an additional servant, and provided her with a carriage.

We must blame Carlyle freely when we find him wrong, that we may praise him fully when we find him right. His patriotism had steadied his politics in the matter of the Crimean War. Declaring Balaklava mud to be but the compendious expression and visibility in miniature of English muddle, he had testified nevertheless, "There is something almost grand in the stubborn thickside patience and persistence of this English People; and I do not question but they will work themselves through in one fashion or another." How could he be less just to the American people? how could he in their dark hour hurl such a missile against them as his deplorable "American Iliad in a Nutshell" (Aug., 1863)—a light and empty nutshell indeed as regarded any kernel of sense or worth, but flung with the fury of a catapult? It was the Nemesis of his aberration on the question of slavery in general. He had fostered error and fondled paradox until he had actually brought himself to see no difference between buying a man like a sheep and hiring him with his own consent for a life-long service. Mournful indeed that he who had so keen an eye for the hero who had passed into the land of shadows should have had none for the hero who confronted him in the flesh as Abraham Lincoln. So vast was the error, that he finally discovered it himself. When Mrs. Charles Lowell, mother of a New England youth fallen in the war, whose biography he had read, came to visit him, he took her by the hand and said, even with tears, "I doubt I have been mistaken."

In November, 1865, Carlyle received the only public honour accepted by him from his own country. He was elected Lord Rector of the University of Edinburgh by the students, in succession to Mr. Gladstone, and by a large majority over Disraeli. He is not wise who disdains such an honour, if it be true that the fate of every country lies in the hands of its citizens under five and twenty. Carlyle certainly did not, for all his disparaging talk. He would not else have faced the very trying ordeal of his

public address, which, as the day of inauguration ap-
proached, became a nightmare to him. Professor Tyndall,
himself on the way to receive an honorary degree,
took charge of him: "kind, cheery, inventive, helpful;
the loyallest son could not have more faithfully striven to
support his father." They left town on March 29, 1866.
Carlyle's own account of his visit to Edinburgh, written
afterwards in his mood of desolation, when the pen was
dropping from his weary hand, is denounced by Professor Masson as "a dull and dismalized blur of the
facts and circumstances." This view is entirely borne
out by Mr. Moncure Conway, who immediately after
the delivery of Carlyle's address (April 2nd) " saw his
countenance as I had never seen it before—without
any trace of spiritual pain." Strange had it been otherwise; he had seen the proudest day of his life;
students and grey-haired men gathered at his feet; listening as he spoke " slowly, connectedly, nobly," " like
children held by a tale of wonderland." His discourse
was like his own deep eye, which, the reporter says, sometimes beat like a pulse, but for the most part looked merely
sedate and kindly. With an occasional flash of eloquence,
but in general with the composure of one who knew that
his work had been weighed in the balance and not found
wanting, he talked to the crowd of young men—such a
crowd as those of which in old time he had himself
formed a portion ; a crowd which, for aught he knew,
might conceal another Carlyle. He could tell them little
that he had not already told ; Cromwell and Goethe came
into his speech as illustrations of his thought, and their
shades upbore the old prophet as Moses was upheld by

Aaron and Hur. He spoke of diligence in its noblest form, diligence to find out the truth; of eloquence and wealth, and what curses they might become; of the mighty changes that were coming over "Oxford and other places that used to seem to lie at anchor in the stream of time;" of the clear, plain, geometric mirror that man's intellect ought to be, and the convexity or concavity that it was; of the priceless worth of bodily and mental sanity, insomuch that even the man of genius, when he had delivered his message, would do well to haste back out of inspiration into health, and regard the real equilibrium as the centre of things. When all was said the students thronged around him, some shedding tears—ominous, prophetic tears ! Carlyle withdrew from the stir to his brother James at Scotsbrig, and continued there, refreshed by quiet and pure air, and rejoiced by affectionate letters from his wife, more demonstrative in her pride than had been her wont. ("I haven't been so fond of everybody since I was a girl.") On the 21st of April, after writing to him, she went out for a drive in the Park. A little dog which accompanied the carriage was run over by another carriage, and slightly hurt. Mrs. Carlyle was out of her brougham almost before it could stop, took the little dog up, and continued her drive. The coachman, receiving no direction from her, and noticing that she never varied her attitude, became alarmed, stopped, and begged a lady to look into the carriage. Jane Carlyle was found dead.

If he could have died in her place, as he would have wished ! No more sorrow then ; no hopeless tears ; no remorseful self-accusation, bitter as the reproach his failing faculties allowed him to cast on others, and hardly more just; chiefest of mercies, no literary executor! She would have guarded his fame; in another sense than that in which she had said it of Irving, " the tongues " would never have been heard. Had Heaven indeed ordered aright? *Peace,* foolish Messieurs!

## CHAPTER IX

" I see his life, as in a map of rivers,
   Through shadows, over rocks, breaking its way
   Until it meet another's, and with that
   Wrestle and tumble o'er a perilous rock
   Bare as Death's shoulder : one of them is lost,
   And a dark haunted flood creeps wailing on
   Into the deadly Styx."

CARLYLE'S life had taken the terrible plunge thus painted by the poet : from the foot of the precipice down which he had been cast he looked up in dumb despair to the height where he was never again to stand. It might have been otherwise had the catastrophe happened some years earlier, when he had strength and spirits for sustained labour. But "Frederick" had exhausted him : his powers of word-painting and of epigram remained unimpaired, but he was now to give lamentable evidence of the decline of judgment and of the faculty of combining diverse elements into a finished work. Sympathy was not wanting to him : it came especially from the highest Lady in the land, graciously and gracefully conveyed through Lady Augusta Stanley. His diaries express his feelings of gratitude for such

condolences, and his equally decided feeling that they
did not profit him. The sympathy of his kindred
seemed more promising: but, after some months' experi-
ment of joint housekeeping, his brother John and he,
with unimpaired esteem and affection, concluded that
they would be better apart. Miss Bromley and other
kind friends invited him to their houses, and he found
some pleasurable excitement in the autumn in joining
"a most feeble committee" formed for the defence of
Governor Eyre. Mill was on the other side; both were
equally wrong; the Government they agreed to abuse
had acted with perfect justice and good sense. The
second Lady Ashburton, who had won Carlyle's wife's
heart as well as his own, urged him to spend the winter
at Mentone, and he departed for her villa on December
22nd, under the affectionate guardianship of Professor
Tyndall. It is to be wished that he had seen more of
Southern Europe. His letters and diaries during the
visit contain exquisite sketches of the minor details of a
panorama whose total impression he thus reproduced in
conversation: "It is a beautiful coast, but very awful:
the great mountains with bare heads and breasts, rugged
and scarred and wrinkled and horrible as the very Witch
of Endor, but clothed over below with flowing garments
of green stretching down to where they dip their feet in
the still waters." Never, he added, had he felt so
solitary and oppressed at heart as when in his lonely
rambles he trod the faded carpeting of those chestnut
woods.

"I was bowed under heavy sorrow, and grief teaches one the
measureless solitude of life, when no comfort or counsel is good for

aught, except what a man can find in himself, and not much there, saving as the conviction is borne in upon him that in mystery and darkness everything is ruled by one most wise and most good, and he learns to say in his heart, 'Thy will be done!' There's not much need of any other prayer but that."

He returned in March, generally benefited by his excursion, but suffering from further failure of digestive power: " Let us be quiet with it—accept it as a means of exit, of which there must always be *some* mode."

One who could have looked into the house of mourning in the summer of 1866 would have seen an old man, " thin, and aged, and sad as Jeremiah, though the red was still bright on his cheek and the blue in his eye," writing what, when it was done, he called " my sacred shrine and religious city of refuge from the bitterness of these sorrows during all the doleful weeks that are past since I took it up ; a kind of devotional thing which softens all grief into tenderness and infinite pity and repentant love, one's whole sad life drowned as if in tears for one, and all the wrath and scorn and other grim elements silently melted away." This was the memoir of his lost wife, to which were subsequently added recollections of Irving and Jeffrey, the tribute to his father written in 1832 and never looked at since, and miscellaneous notes, chiefly on Wordsworth and Southey : the whole forming the two volumes of " Reminiscences " which his executor thought it decent to publish almost before he was cold in his grave.

Most autobiographies (Mill's a signal exception) have been written or coloured for effect. Carlyle's is the most artless of all his writings. He wrote like a man in a dream, and what he had written soon became to him dim and eerie as a dream. His chapter on Irving fills 272 pages octavo: some time afterwards he needed to be reminded that he had written it. His book was never meant for publication. " Is not all this appointed by me rigorously to the fire? " he says in a passage *omitted* by Mr. Froude. " Somehow it solaces me to have written it." It is a soliloquy, a sad crooning, interrupted with gusts of wail, and but for these—

> " A low sleepy tune,
> An outworn and unused monotony,
> Such as our country gossips sing and spin,
> Till they almost forget they live."

Had his literary faculty been wakeful, it would have admonished him that what he wrote would defeat its own end. He wished, as far as he wished anything consciously beyond the relief of his burdened heart, to give vent to his own remorse for every neglect of which he could fancy himself guilty towards his wife, to atone for every pang of hers unexpectedly revealed to him by her diary, and to paint her as an ideal woman. He has missed his mark from overdrawing his bow. We become unjustly sceptical and justly bored. Far more effect would have been produced by a few grave and measured words. The account of Jeffrey is bright; that of Irving prolix and rambling; the lament for his father has been already characterized. One faculty alone survives: the power of etching vignettes of still or human life remains wholly unimpaired, and what a power! The literary connoisseur's eyes gleam when he meets a

Carlyle, as the eyes of the connoisseur of art when he meets a Rembrandt.

Carlyle's life is full of irony, and nothing in it is more quaintly lamentable than that in this book, undertaken partly as an anodyne, partly as a penance, he should have given more pain and committed more offences than in all the rest of his writings. The untruths, the injustices, the gratuitous wounds throughout these unhappy volumes are too numerous to be overlooked, too flagrant to be forgiven were it not so certain that they arose from some cause independent of the writer's will, and that they were never given to the world with his consent. There was not another man of letters of his standing whose life had been so honourably free from miserable feuds. No man had less resented attack, or estrangement yet more grievous. We have seen with what pleasure he cited Mill's name for praise after their alienation; we find his censure of Croker and William Taylor leavened with all the commendation he could see it just to bestow. "I never heard him tell a malicious story or say a malicious word of any human being," deposes Mr. Froude, an authority on this point, as Mr. Morison remarks with cutting sarcasm. The explanation must be found in his mental state at the time. He wrote as in a dream, sounding the depths of his memory for reminiscences, and transcribing rather than composing. The impressions made upon perceptive powers like his were wonderfully sharp and durable. It will have been noticed with what slight variation of language he repeats the same story or the same idea at widely different periods of his life. Every impression came back to him exactly as he had first received it, and in the paralysis of his judgment he lacked the power to correct, to mitigate, or to combine. This apology for Carlyle does not mend the mischief he unwittingly did. If the sufferers refuse to forgive, it must be owned that they are fully within their right. But if justice demands this acknowledgment, it no less demands the recognition that Carlyle was the chief sufferer by his own bitterness. "Why," he exclaims, most touchingly, "why do we not always love, and why is the loved soul shut out from us by poor obstructions, that we see it only in glimpses, or at best look at it from a prison grate, and into a prison grate?"

If indignation must have course, it will not die away for want of an object. How came Carlyle's trusted friend and literary executor to publish this book with hardly any retrenchment or alteration, in defiance of Carlyle's most positive injunctions? About these injunctions there is no mistake—here they are :

"I still mainly mean to burn this book before my own departure, but feel that I shall always have a kind of grudge to do it, and an indolent excuse, 'Not yet ; wait, any day that can be done !' and then it is possible the thing may be left behind me, legible to interested survivors—friends only, I will hope, and with worthy curiosity, not unworthy !

"In which event, I solemnly forbid them, each and all, to publish this bit of writing as it stands here ; and warn them that without fit editing no part of it should be printed (nor so far as I can order shall ever be) ; and that the fit editing of perhaps nine-tenths of it will, after I am gone, have become impossible.

"T. C., 28 July, 1866."

Five years afterwards, Carlyle, who had not since
looked at his manuscript, placed it in the hands of him
in whose judgment and affection he most confided.   Mr.
Froude says that he persuaded Carlyle to consent to the
publication of " the greater part of the memoir."   Carlyle's niece disbelieves this, but granting it, Mr. Froude
himself says, " It was understood that certain parts were
to be omitted."   When, however, Professor Norton came
to examine the manuscript, he found that the only
omissions of any importance were some pages of a diary
of Mrs. Carlyle's, and the postscript which disclosed Mr.
Froude's disregard of his friend's injunction.   It is difficult to reconcile his conduct with the stern love of truth
by which he professes himself to have been actuated.
In that case why suppress the postscript ?   Why conceal
the breach of his understanding with Carlyle ?   Why,
with the fullest discretion to omit, give currency to so
many things of which he must have suspected the
accuracy, which he must have known would give pain to
the innocent ?   Whence the innumerable errors in his
edition ?   Was it love of truth, or love of sensation ?
*Avec cette sauce là on mangerait son père.*

Carlyle was an exception to Anthony Trollope's maxim
that a man does not roar very long, if he roars very loud.
In 1867 he published in *Macmillan's Magazine* his
" Shooting Niagara," a belated Latter-Day Pamphlet,
called forth by the alarm with which he regarded the
extension of the franchise in that year, but rambling into
extraneous topics, and liable to his own criticism upon
Coleridge, that he skirted the desert he should have
crossed.   The advice to the aristocracy to abstain from

political action is, from his own point of view, the worst
he could have given. Hatred of parliaments had become
a monomania with him. Mill's "Liberty" excited his
especial wrath. When he first read it he turned round
upon Mr. Larkin, who happened to be by, and shook
him (figuratively) as a terrier shakes a rat. As if poor
Mr. Larkin had written "Liberty"; as if, while in Carlyle's employment, he had any liberty to write about!
The ground of this passion is difficult to discover; for
the liberties which Mill thought should be given were
mostly those which Carlyle had already taken. What is
truly remarkable is that this golden little book contains,
*mutatis mutandis*, one of the best descriptions of
Carlyle's own mission and influence: as will appear
by substituting "Carlyle" for "Rousseau" in the para-
graph of chapter ii. beginning, "Thus, in the eighteenth
century." Mill's point of view might have reconciled
some of Carlyle's young followers, who, not content with
stimulus, craved for system. Some of the shepherdless
migrated to Comte, whom Carlyle, overlooking the fact
that Comte had excommunicated sidereal physics, described as a man holding a lantern to the stars. Darwin
pleased him no better, though bringing support to some
of his most cherished ideas. He had been preaching
the Survival of the Fittest all his life, only in another
language. He might also have remembered that Goethe
had been an Evolutionist. Thirty years before he had
apprehended the drift of Herder's speculations in this
direction, which, coming from such a man, had filled him
with strange dubieties. He thought he scented irreligion:
and in fact the Evolution which on the lips of a Tyndall

seems the scientific demonstration of Carlyle's Pantheistic Theism comes very differently from Carlyle's especial aversion, a merely mechanical natural philosopher. He could not read "Cosmos." "What does Humboldt see in the universe? Nothing but an old marine store-shop collection of things putrifying and rotting, under certain forces and laws. A most melancholy picture of things!" In the same conversation he complained that Germany had for a quarter of a century produced no original thought : his Argus vision had failed to discover Schopenhauer.

Carlyle's last literary labour of importance was his sketch of the Early Kings of Norway, completed in February, 1872, and published in *Fraser* in January and March, 1875: his inquiry into the authenticity of the portraits of John Knox appeared in the same magazine in the following April. Both, especially the latter, show much of his old fire, but he could no longer use his right hand, and found the expression of his thought much impeded by dictation. The other public utterances of these latter days were mainly political. In November, 1870, he addressed a most powerful letter to the *Times* on the Franco-German conflict. A letter on the Turkish war in 1877 enriched the platform with that serviceable catchword, "the unspeakable Turk." That Carlyle was not impervious to new light in public matters appears from a palinodia in one of his letters to Emerson. "Could any Friedrich Wilhelm now, or Friedrich, or most perfect governor you could hope to realize, guide forward what is America's essential task at present faster or more completely than anarchic America herself is now doing?"

The last book that appeared under his name is the
philippic against "promoterism," written in 1872, published in 1882 as "The Last Words of Thomas Carlyle."
As Napoleon's last murmur had been *Tête d'Armée*, so
Carlyle passed from the world repeating, "Honesty,
honesty."

Honours came unsought to Carlyle in the latter years
of his life. In 1874 he received the Prussian order Pour
le Mérite, founded by Frederick, perhaps the soundest
criterion of merit in Europe. At the end of the same
year, Disraeli, then Prime Minister, surprised him by the
offer of the Grand Cross of the Bath, never before conferred by the Queen except for direct services to the State.
The offer of a pension was added. Up to this time
Disraeli, in Carlyle's eyes, had possessed but one redeem-
ing virtue: he was not Gladstone. "A mouthing verba-
list and juggling adventurer." Now Carlyle could but
"truly admire the magnanimity of Dizzy in regard to me.
If there is anything of scurrility anywhere chargeable
against me, he is the subject of it; and yet see, here he
comes with a pan of hot coals for my guilty head." He
could, nevertheless, only assure the Premier that "his
splendid and generous proposals must not take effect;"
that "titles of honour would be an encumbrance, not a
furtherance;" that "money had become in this latter
time amply abundant, even superabundant." With con-
summate delicacy, he delayed this reply until he knew
the decision of Tennyson, to whom a baronetcy had been
offered, lest the Laureate should be thought to have
merely followed his lead. Pious and ingenious diplomacy
afterwards arranged an interview between him and Dis-

raeli, and he had to tell the statesman that if he had
known him sooner he might have abused him less.   His
eightieth birthday, Dec. 4, 1875, brought numerous testi-
monies of admiring sympathy, including a telegram from
the literary men of Germany, headed by Ranke ; a letter
from Prince Bismarck; and a medallion portrait in gold by
Boehm, the offering of more than a hundred friends and
students, mostly of distinguished standing in the intellectual world, who had obeyed the thoughtful prompting
of Mr. Laurenson, an admirer in the remote Shetlands,
and of Professor Masson.

The palsy of Carlyle's hand had ere this closed one
vent for his morbid moods, his diary, a sad depository of
the sorrows real and imaginary which compassed him
round about ; yet, besides its service as a safety-valve, not
lacking a final cause.   It confutes the heresy of the elder
Henry James—(*ein wunderlicher Kauz* who tried to persuade him that they were both of them dead, but, producing neither airs from heaven nor blasts from hell in
evidence of his spectrality, was necessitated to " blow his
bellows elsewhere ")—that "he valued truth and good
as a painter does his pigments, not for themselves, but for
their effects."   The seal of sincerity is impressed on all
these weary pages, designed for no eyes but his own.
The last years of his widowerhood, nevertheless, were far
more cheerful than the first.   Professor Norton, who saw
much of him at this period, returned to America with a
different report from Emerson's.   Emerson had named
Carlyle's conversation as the second of the three things
which had most impressed him in Europe.   Norton,
though finding that his talk had lost nothing of its raci-

ness and vigour, thought his most striking characteristics
not those of the intellect, but of the heart. Asperity and
petulance were softened, if not subdued; he could flash
into scorn on occasion, but rarely stormed, denounced,
or preached; never put on the air of a prophet, and spoke
much too slightingly of his own writings. He was full
of sweet thoughtfulness for children, and his ways with
them were most gentle and gracious. If he did denounce
anything not plainly base, the denunciation, says Mr.
Allingham, "generally ended in a laugh, the heartiest in
the world, at his own ferocity. Those who have not heard
that laugh will never know what Carlyle's talk was."
Had he not himself said in "Sartor Resartus," "How
much lies in laughter, the cipher-key wherewith we decipher
the whole man!" Emerson's last visit to England (1872–73)
gave him great pleasure, but he was puzzled as well as
pleased. He found his old friend the same incorrigible
sinner, hardened in faith and hope. "It's a very
striking and curious spectacle to behold a man in these
days so confidently cheerful as Emerson!" He greatly
enjoyed Ruskin's later writings: "If he had but twenty
or thirty good years before him to shoot his swift, singing
arrows at the Python, he'd make the monster turn up his
white belly at last."

In his latter days Carlyle depended much on the affectionate care of his niece Mary Aitken, who came to live
with him, and was destined to be not only the stay of his
old age, but the faithful guardian of his memory when
he should be no more. His figure was not unfamiliar to
Londoners, especially in his own neighbourhood. Clad
in long-skirted brown coat, with soft black or in summer

a straw hat, with soft leather shoes, always tied, and in doubtful weather a mackintosh (he would never carry an umbrella), he walked twice a day on the Chelsea Embankment, or in Battersea Park, alone or one of a small group. He would sometimes stray further than he could easily return on foot, and passengers in Chelsea omnibuses became familiar with his rugged face and strange double look, half fiercely alert, half dreamy and far-away. He would frequently sit in his little garden, wearing a slaty-grey dressing-gown, reading or smoking in the company of his good cat Tib, immortalized in Mrs. Allingham's sketch of her master. His circumstances were now opulent; his name seldom appeared in subscriptions, but he gave largely in secret; he could, as he did, urge that a legacy intended for himself should be bestowed on the Literary Fund, or on the testator's impoverished relatives, "the mode of disposal which would enrich me most." While arranging his affairs he had bequeathed the books used in his work on "Cromwell" and "Frederick" to Harvard College; unexpressed amends, it can hardly be doubted, for his misjudgment of the American Civil War. He also gave, by a deed secretly executed in his lifetime, the income of Craigenputtock to the University of Edinburgh, to found for poor students ten bursaries to be known, in memory of his wife and her family, as the John Welsh bursaries. Five were to be bestowed irrevocably for mathematical proficiency, the other five for proficiency in classics so long as the University should see fit. "So may a little trace of help, to the young heroic soul struggling for what is highest, spring from this poor arrangement and bequest ; may it run for ever if it can, as a thread of pure water from the Scottish rocks, tinkling into its little basin by the thirsty wayside, for those whom it veritably belongs to. Amen."

The little rill began to tinkle on February 5, 1881. On that day Thomas Carlyle died, his last words, "Good-bye." His worth demanded Westminster for his place of sepulture, but his wish had decreed Ecclefechan. There he was laid among his kindred, on February 10th. It was emblematical of the world's judgment on him that the foremost men at his grave, Lecky and Tyndall, were the foremost men of Ireland, the land he had rebuked so sternly and pitied so much. Sleet and rain beat hard upon the mourners, but all was sunshine at the last.

# CHAPTER X.

" For this reason, that thou art the King,
And only blind from sheer supremacy,
One avenue was shaded from thine eyes,
Through which I wandered to eternal truth."

THE biographer of a great imperfect man, if no bolder than an angel, must be grateful to old Oceanus for this hint of an apology so nicely adapted to his own case. He must be sensible that, from no fault of his own, his attitude towards his hero, as he slaps and strokes, partakes somewhat of the nature of impertinence. " There, I must say, you acted handsomely—there you took a wrong turn, I wish you had had me at your elbow—those are fine sentiments, but *were* the nuisances in the bed? or did you bring them up with you from Scotland?—what possessed you to write that vociferous pamphlet, not the least sentence in which I could have written to save my life?" There is no remedy; moral and literary judgment is an incumbent duty, and the biographer can only fall back upon the "one avenue," and hope that it may have been disclosed to him. Guides unknown to his predecessors have come forward in the shape of Carlyle's early letters, and the correspondence with Emerson and

Goethe. Professor Masson and Professor Norton have delivered their verdicts; Mr. J. C. Morison has summed up the whole case in an essay which would almost have superseded the need for anything further, if his plan had included biography; the heart of Carlyle's mystery is in every way riper for plucking than it was.

"I remember," says Leopold Schefer, writing at the end of a long literary life, "entering into Petrarch's garden at Arquá. The pomegranate trees stooped down with their fruit, greeting me. I broke off the crown from a fruit, gathered it, and tasted the crystallized seeds, but they were yet green and sour. Dear biographer, I, too, have been gathered, tasted, criticized too soon; and it needs a man like you to take me like a pomegranate into his hand, and say how the core, by this time mellowed, pleases him."

The reader himself shall taste the seeds in the shape of a few of the most seminal passages expressive of the vital essence of Carlyle's teaching.

On the highest of all subjects Carlyle is as explicit as could possibly be desired. Speaking to his academical subjects, the young students at Edinburgh University, to whom he stood for the moment in the relation of a Shepherd and Bishop of souls, he said in carefully chosen words—

"I believe you will find in all histories that that [religion] has been at the head and foundation of them all, and that no nation that did not contemplate this wonderful Universe with an awe-stricken and reverential feeling that there was a great unknown, omnipotent, and all-wise and all-virtuous Being, superintending all men in it and all interests in it—no nation ever came to very much, nor did any man either, who forgot that."

They who add aught to or diminish aught from this

simple faith cannot claim Carlyle as theirs.   His conception of Deity, alternately Pantheistic or Theistic, as either
view may seem for the moment more in harmony with
the reverence which it is his constant purpose to express,
never displays the least tendency to Polytheism.  His "Hero
Worship" is something totally different from the veneration of saints or the cult of Positivism; to him the service
of man is worship indeed, but of God, not of humanity.
Two great corollaries from his belief we can but barely
state, for their discussion would require a volume.  "The
Natural *is* the Supernatural."   "All History is a Bible."
On personal immortality he is silent; or rather, by
treating Time as an illusion, he sinks the question beyond
the brief fathom-line of thought.   But he would have
treated the idea of making the expectation of it a moral
sanction with contempt "acrid as the spirit of sloes and
copperas."

On Man Carlyle is equally explicit, but his estimate
necessarily shifts according as he looks upon Man in
himself, or in relation to the things above him and around
him.   From the former point of view, no language can
too grandly describe the grandeur of Mankind—

"Thus, like some wild-flaming, wild-thundering train of Heaven's
Artillery, does this mysterious Mankind thunder and flame, in long-
drawn, quick-succeeding grandeur, through the unknown Deep.
Thus, like a God-created fire-breathing Spirit-host, we emerge
from the Inane; haste stormfully across the astonished Earth, then
plunge again into the Inane.   Earth's mountains are levelled and
her seas filled up in our passage; can the Earth, which is but dead
and a vision, resist Spirits which have reality and are alive?   On
the hardest adamant some footprint of ours is stamped in; the last
ear of the host will read traces of the earliest van.   But whence?—

O Heaven, whither? Sense knows not; Faith knows not; only that it is through Mystery to Mystery, from God and to God."

But if Man in himself is great, his relation to the Universe is a humble one, even as he fathoms its secrets and learns its laws—

"The course of Nature's phases in this our little fraction of a Planet is partially known to us, but who knows what deeper courses these depend on; what infinitely larger Cycle of causes our little Epicycle revolves on? To the Minnow every cranny and pebble, and quality and accident, of its little native brook may have become familiar; but does the Minnow understand the Ocean Tides and periodic Currents, the Trade-winds, and Monsoons, and Moon's Eclipses; by all which the condition of its little Creek is regulated, and may from time to time (unmiraculously enough) be quite over-set and reversed? Such a minnow is Man; his Creek this planet Earth; his Ocean the immeasurable All; his Monsoons and periodic Currents the mysterious Course of Providence through Aeons of Aeons."

Carlyle's ethics are also in substance very clear, although, as he was by no means logical, and never cared " to make a system refutation-tight," it would be easy to convict him of apparent inconsistencies. One of his most admiring and intelligent followers, for example, has criticized him for teaching that Might makes Right, and the letter of the record is against him, though he protested with perfect sincerity that he had intended the exact contrary. In all such cases, the general spirit of his teaching must be looked to, and then the only question will be as to the relative importance of his ideas in his own mind. One would have agreed with Professor Minto that he attached chief importance to the performance of Duty, but he

himself declared in his old age that he regarded Truth
as the Alpha and Omega of his message. Speaking of
his books, he said—

"I've had but one thing to say from beginning to end of them,
and that was, that there's no other reliance for this world or any
other but just the Truth, and that if men did not want to be damned
to all eternity they had best give up lying and all kinds of falsehood;
that the world was far gone already through lying, and that there's
no hope for it but just so far as men find out and believe the Truth,
and match their lives to it. But on the whole the world has gone
on lying worse than ever."

As corollary from this paramount importance of Truth
Carlyle is continually insisting on the paramount importance of Fact, the necessity of accepting the phenomena of
the Universe for what they are, not taking them for what
we should like them to be—

"We perceive that this man [Frederick] was far indeed from
trying to deal swindler-like with the facts around him; that he
honestly recognized said facts wherever they disclosed themselves,
and was very anxious also to ascertain their existence where still
hidden and dubious. For he knew well how entirely inexorable is
the nature of facts, whether recognized or not, ascertained or not;
how vain all cunning of diplomacy, management and sophistry, to
save any mortal who does not stand on the truth of things from
sinking in the long run."

It lay in Carlyle's temperament that he generally
seemed to assume that facts must needs be less delightful than appearances, instead of more so, as well may
happen. He thus exaggerated the arduousness of Duty,
a mistake in a moralist. His absolute disinterestedness
was alone a sufficient deterrent to many. " A sad creed

this of the King's," he says, ironically, "he had to do his duty without fee or reward." Perhaps the most energetic expression of his ideal of disinterested duty is the on-slaught on Benthamism in "Hero Worship," which, as Carlyle pronounced the word "beggarlier," brought Mill to his feet with an emphatic No!—

"What is the chief end of man here below? Mahomet has answered this question in a way that might put some of us to shame. He does not, like a Bentham or Paley, take Right and Wrong, and calculate the profit and loss, ultimate pleasure of the one and of the other; and summing all up by addition and sub-traction into a net result, ask you, Whether on the whole the Right does not preponderate considerably? No: it is not *better* to do one than the other, the one is to the other as life is to death, as Heaven is to Hell! The one must in nowise be done, the other in nowise left undone. Ye shall not measure them; they are incom-mensurable: the one is death eternal to a man, the other is life eternal. Benthamee Utility, virtue by Profit and Loss; reducing this God's world to a dead brute steam-engine, the infinite celestial Soul of Man to a kind of Hay-balance for weighing hay and thistles on, pleasures and pains on :—if you ask me which gives, Mahomet or they, the beggarlier and the falser view of Man and his Destinies in this Universe, I will answer, It is not Mahomet!"

As from allegiance to Truth Carlyle deduced loyalty to Fact as a paramount obligation, so his disinterested conception of Duty implied the intrinsic worth of Work, recompensed or in this world wageless—

"All true work is sacred; in all true work, even if but true hand-labour, there is something of divineness. O brother, if this is not worship, then I say the more pity for worship, for this is the noblest thing yet discovered under God's sky. Who art thou who complainest of thy life of toil? Complain not. Look up, my wearied brother: see thy fellow workmen there in God's eternity;

surviving there, they alone surviving; sacred band of the immortals, celestial body-guard of the Empire of Mankind. Even in the weak human memory they survive as saints, as heroes, as gods; they alone surviving, peopling they alone the unmeasured solitudes of time. To thee Heaven, though severe, is not unkind; Heaven is kind; as a noble mother, as that Spartan mother saying, when she gave her son his shield, *With this, my son, or upon it.* Thou, too, shalt return home in honour, to thy far distant home in honour, doubt it not, if in the battle thou keep thy shield."

What can be added to this? Only that Carlyle had no idea of offering any vulgar bribe to his strenuous workman, and that, with him, "eternity," "thy distant home," and similar shadowings forth of the unspeakable must not be taken in the sense which it is customary to attach to them.

Some of Carlyle's followers have prepared a pitfall for his fame by staking his reputation for insight upon the literal fulfilment of his political prophecies. If interest continue to be paid upon the Three Per Cents, then the Lord hath not spoken by Thomas Carlyle! This is to restore the mechanical definition of prophecy which he banished. His application of ethics to politics has perpetual value, so long as he adheres to his first principles. The most important of these is that the Rights of Man are altogether subordinate to the Duties of Man. "Would in this world of ours is a mere zero to Should." In the sphere of practical politics we must discriminate between the strictly political department of his ideas, and the social and economical. The moral influence of the former, in so far as it tended to lift men above party, and to fix attention on what was really vital in institutions, discarding the unessential or obsolete, was of supreme worth. In practical suggestion he is weak: " his hero-king," says Professor Minto, " means in practice an accidentally good and able man in a series of indifferent or bad despots," as we have seen in the case of Francia. It is nevertheless most seasonable as a protest against the besetting evil of this age, the universal cowardice of governments. Carlyle's panegyrics of masterful, strong-handed, unscrupulous authority, are not bread to live by, but tonics to reinvigorate the system. They are also too contrary to the spirit of the age to be mischievous— massy stones athwart the current, able at most to pro-voke the waters into foam. His social doctrines, on the contrary, have the spirit of the age with them. State interference is more and more solicited, and though its dangers are undeniable, it seems to be instinctively felt that it is an alternative to social convulsion.

Carlyle's views of human destiny are less gloomy than they sometimes seem. "This world is built, not on falsehood and jargon, but on truth and reason." He does not ridicule progress, nor despair of it ; but merely denies that it is taking place in his own day, and disputes its uniformity and continuity. He believes in cycles of progress, ending at a higher point than they began, and begetting new cycles destined to engender new growth upward and new dying down. The aphorism that "pro-gress is not in a straight line, but in a spiral," condenses his views—

" Find Mankind where thou wilt, thou findest it in living move-ment, in progress faster or slower : the Phœnix soars aloft, hovers with outstretched wings, filling Earth with her music ; or, as now, she sinks, and with spheral swan-song immolates herself in flame, that she may soar the higher and sing the clearer."

" I have no notion of a truly great man that could not be all sorts of men." This bold saying of Carlyle's is refuted by his own weakness in science and art. His interest in science, as in poetry, was solely ethical. If he could connect a scientific discovery or hypothesi with what he deemed a truth in religion or morals, he was delighted ; if, like the Darwinian theory, it came in company with an unwelcome conclusion, he was disgusted ; but he admits his indifference to even such a hero of research as Faraday, if his discoveries had no visible influence on human conduct or welfare. It was the same with art : cathedral architecture impressed him as the incarnation of religious feeling, but his taste in painting was that of any Annandale peasant. This insensibility to pictorial art was accompanied by the most wonderful gift of word-painting, the most graphic and intense touch in hitting off a likeness, the most exquisite sensibility to the form, colour, and sentiment of a landscape. These pages are already thick-sown with examples, but yet another may be cited in illustration of his gift of imaginative landscape, his power of creating a scene in his own mind. " Teufelsdröckh emerges (we know not well whence) in the solitude of the North Cape, on that June midnight," to gaze on the Midnight Sun—

" Silence as of death : nothing but the granite cliffs ruddy-tinged, the peaceable gurgling of that slow-heaving Polar Ocean, over which in the utmost North the great Sun hangs low and lazy, as if he too were slumbering. Yet is his cloud-couch wrought of crimson cloth of gold ; yet does his light stream over the mirror of waters, like a tremulous fire pillar, shooting downwards towards the abyss, and hide itself under my feet. In such moments, Solitude also is invaluable, for who would speak, or be looked on, when behind him lies all Europe and Africa, fast asleep, except the watchmen ; and before him the silent Immensity, and Palace of the Eternal, whereof our Sun is but a porch-lamp ? "

Of Carlyle's literary genius hardly anything more need be said here. His supremacy is attested by the fact that he is one of the very few in whose hands language is wholly flexible and fusible. The same may be said of the one Englishman of this century who is fully his peer in literary genius, Shelley, and of no other. Shelley works his will with language gracefully, as one guides a spirited steed : Carlyle with convulsive effort, as one hammers a red-hot bar, but in both cases the end is achieved. The two should be painted, like Plato and Verulam in the Palace of Art, as twin masters of speech, if such masters could have pupils. But such power is not granted for the expression of vain and shallow thought, and whoever shares their gift will stand by their side.

Nor does Carlyle's character as a man need much further elucidation. There is, on the whole, but one way to understand him. "You must love him, ere to you he will seem worthy of your love "—

> "All bright endowments of a noble mind
> They, who with joy behold them, soonest find ;
> And better none its stains of frailty know
> Than they who fain would see it white as snow."

It is nevertheless some help towards apprehension to compare him with the great men of former generations. He evidently saw, and saw truly, some of his own lineaments in the countenances of Johnson, Richter, and Burns. But he can be only adequately compared with the Prophets. The much that is tragically strong is very like Dante, the little that is tragically weak is very like Rousseau. But Dante had little laughter in him, and Rousseau none. Dante's dumb wilderness and Rousseau's howling wilderness are in Carlyle enriched with every kind of growth by subterranean lakes and up-bubbling springs of humour. He might have said with Johnson's friend : " I tried to be a philosopher, but, I don't know how, cheerfulness was always breaking in." No writer of our time so overflows with genuine fun as this outwardly grim and sardonic personage ; no one since Aristophanes has so inextricably interwoven drollery and poetry ; no one, on the whole, has used his gift more genially. He could blast when he saw fit. Of one praying unctuously he said, " That man is asking for treacle ; he will get brimstone." But he is indulgent to mere human frailty, unless working mischief in high places, or flown with insolence and wine. How good-natured his farewell to Jeshurun waxen lean and not a kick left in him !—

"Whether the poor Wilhelmus did not still, by secret channels, occasionally get some slight wetting of vinous or alcoholic liquor— now grown, in a manner, indispensable to the poor man ?—Jocelin hints not ; one knows not how to hope, what to hope ! But if he did, it was in silence and in darkness ; with an ever-present feeling that teetotalism was his only true course."

On what Carlyle has done for the Past and the Present there can be little serious difference of opinion: it remains for inquiry how far these services will carry his name into the future. A great contemporary, James Martineau, thinks that he will survive, but not quite as he intended. "As a revolutionary or pentecostal power on the sentiments of Englishmen his influence is perhaps nearly spent; and, like the romantic school of Germany, will descend from the high level of faith to the tranquil honours of literature." This was written in 1856. Dr. Martineau is one of the few men of our age who have earned "the liberty of prophesying," but this prediction awaits fulfilment still. Much of "Past and Present" and "Chartism" is, no doubt, of merely temporary application, but "Sartor Resartus" deals with the themes that interested Job, and we should no more expect it to be studied in a purely literary point of view than that Scripture, which also is a literary work. It will be read as a gospel, or not at all. "Hero Worship" is a link between "Sartor" and Carlyle's more secular writings— a prophecy, but also a gallery of biographical portraiture, which no student of the men depicted by it can neglect. In "Cromwell," "Frederick," and the majority of his Essays, Carlyle has provided for his own renown in the same manner, by linking his name to names already immortal: he will be forgotten when they are forgotten, and not till then. Sterling is another kind of spirit, but Carlyle's life of him, apart from its charm of execution, will always be indispensable for the intellectual history of the age. There remains "The French Revolution," a work which, if we regard it as a history, marks an epoch in historical composition from which literary annalists will date ; which, as a poem, should not be less certain of immortality than its weaker, though strong, forerunner, Lucan's Pharsalia.

But it is not as man of letters that we would chiefly think of Carlyle, nor is it in his study that we would part with him. Great and deathless writer as he was, he will be honoured by posterity for his influence on human life, rather than for his supremacy as a literary artist. "The way to test how much he has left his country," says a great writer of another country, "were to consider, or try to consider, for a moment, the array of British thought, the resultant *ensemble* of the last fifty years, as existing to-day, but with Carlyle left out. It would be like an army with no artillery." The true legend for his monument is the dying witness of John Sterling : "Towards England no man has been and done like you."

THE END.

# INDEX.